"Tut-tut," Jader said. "Naked in the kitchen?"

Standing up straight, Ellen grasped each end of the towel and stretched it across her breasts. Now at least the front of her was concealed from his view, she thought with relief—then realized that the towel barely skimmed her hips.

"Vertical," Jader said.

She looked blankly up at him. "What?"

"If you hold the towel vertically rather than horizontally, it'll cover the front of you—all of you," he explained.

Ellen's pink cheeks burned crimson. "Oh—yes," she said, and made a hasty, fumbled, but far more respectable arrangement. "What are you doing here?" she demanded.

"I missed you," Jader said dryly. "What the hell do you think I'm doing here?"

ELIZABETH OLDFIELD's writing career started as a teenage hobby, when she had articles published. However, on her marriage the creative instinct was diverted into the production of a daughter and son. A decade later, when her husband's job took them to Singapore, she resumed writing, and she had her first romance accepted in 1982. She and her husband live in London, and Elizabeth travels widely to authenticate the background of her books.

His Sleeping Partner

ELIZABETH OLDFIELD

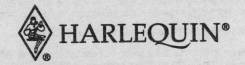

HARLEQUIN®

TORONTO • NEW YORK • LONDON
AMSTERDAM • PARIS • SYDNEY • HAMBURG
STOCKHOLM • ATHENS • TOKYO • MILAN • MADRID
PRAGUE • WARSAW • BUDAPEST • AUCKLAND

ISBN 0-373-80525-X

HIS SLEEPING PARTNER

First North American Publication 2000.

Copyright © 1996 by Elizabeth Oldfield.

CHAPTER ONE

IT WAS instant recognition.

Ellen emerged into the arrivals hall, looked through the flotilla of crazily waving name cards, beyond the massed heads of the expectant crowd, and saw him. Jader de Sa Moreira. She stopped dead. Almost ten years had passed since they had last met and then their association had been brief, so for her gaze to arrow directly to him seemed uncanny. An against-all-the-odds fluke.

Or, on second thoughts, perhaps not. Even if there had been no necessity for her to search out her host, she might well have *noticed* him, Ellen thought wryly. As other women around her were noticing him. His height—a virile six feet something—plus his formal appearance in a slate-grey three-piece business suit and pristine white shirt made him different from the waiting hordes. Though it was his cool, commanding stance, allied with a touch of arrogance, which set him apart.

Ellen's fingers instinctively tightened around the bar of the luggage trolley. The cool was deceptive. Jader de Sa Moreira possessed an internal combustion which could ignite with explosive effect—and heaven help anyone caught in the blast.

As she looked at him, the Brazilian suddenly smiled—a crooked, fetching smile which warmed his deep-set brown eyes. Her grip on the pushbar eased and Ellen smiled back. Whilst his invitation to Rio was a clear-cut gesture of reconciliation, memories of their last meeting had still made her a little apprehensive. But for no reason.

'Hello,' Ellen mouthed, and wiggled her fingers.

Jader shot a hasty look to right and left, as if uncertain whether she was speaking to him, then nodded.

Easing back into the procession of arriving passengers, Ellen trundled her trolley along the roped-off channel. After an eleven-and-a-half-hour overnight flight, and at eight o'clock in the morning, the pace was shambling and slow. She glanced back at Jader. Although he had yet to make a move to greet her, he continued to smile and, she realised, his eyes were flickering over her in obvious male interest.

Ellen hauled the slipping strap of her hefty camera bag higher onto her shoulder. Her mane of long fair hair and willowy figure often drew masculine glances, yet she had not expected this. It had never occurred to her that she might appeal to *him* in a sexual way. A grin glimmered. Yet the idea was…intriguing.

Ellen reached the end of the rope and, when her host remained stubbornly immobile—did the macho psyche of the Latin American male insist that she must approach him?—manoeuvred her trolley around. She pushed forward in his direction. With thick, dark, wavy hair, a Roman nose and clean-cut jaw, he packed an undeniable physical punch. Ten years ago, Jader de Sa Moreira had been an almost pretty young man, she recalled; however, she preferred the sharper angles and leaner planes to his face which maturity had bestowed.

As Ellen drew closer, the rhythm of her heartbeat quickened. His dark brown eyes had locked onto hers and in them she saw not just sexual attraction but something deeper. Far deeper. She saw the dawning awareness that here was a kindred spirit, a soul mate. And, although it

perplexed and bewildered, Ellen felt an answering emotion. Their eyes held. She walked on. Airport noise and
bustle dwindled, other people faded, and by the time she
arrived in front of him only the two of them existed.

'Made it,' Ellen announced, pink-cheeked, breathless
and full of a nerve-tingling sense of anticipation.

Jader arched a black slash of a brow. 'A determined
lady,' he said.

As his looks hit hard in her solar plexus, so did his
voice. He had a low, smooth baritone and, because he had
studied at Cambridge and later spent a couple of years
gaining work experience in the States, spoke perfect English with a murderously sexy accent.

'Always,' she told him.

Jader looked amused. 'So—what happens next?' he enquired, but then abruptly he leaned forward, his dark eyes
narrowed and he muttered what sounded like an oath in
Portuguese. 'It's you!'

Ellen's spine stiffened. Indignation pinched at her lips.
She had believed, first, that he had smiled in welcome and
out of friendship, and, second, that he had been interested
in her—Ellen Blanchard, his guest. But all he had been
interested in was some unknown, anonymous, arrived-
from-anywhere blonde in a petunia-pink T-shirt and faded
blue jeans. Lust had reigned supreme and as for any fusion
of souls—that had been the bizarre concoction of a travel-
worn and jet-lagged mind!

'You thought I was attempting to pick you up?' she
demanded.

Jader spread his hands. 'Well…yes.'

'Zeroing in on complete and utter strangers in order to
fix an assignation is not my style,' Ellen informed him
witheringly.

His mouth tweaked at one corner. 'Then maybe you

should try it some time? I can guarantee you'll have one heck of a success rate.'

'You'd have succumbed?' she enquired, not sure whether she felt bitingly contemptuous or sneakily pleased. 'But I might've been a psychopath. Or a serial killer. Or—'

'A vampire out for a quick bite?' Jader suggested, when she cast wildly around for another idea. 'Anything is possible. However, I wouldn't have succumbed, not least because my sole purpose in being at the airport is to meet you. I apologise most sincerely for my mistake,' he carried on, without missing a beat, 'but you've changed.'

Ellen gave a small, taut smile. The years had altered her in a number of ways. 'You mean that last time we met I wore a brace on my teeth and was still in the process of shedding the final few pounds of puppy fat?' she said.

'Plus your hair had been hacked short, your clothes were relentlessly baggy and you made not even a passing stab at make-up.'

She frowned, surprised that he should remember her in such detail. Unflattering detail. 'I was being determinedly plain Jane,' she defended.

'Why would you do that?' Jader enquired.

Ellen tossed silky wheat-blonde curls back from her shoulders. 'I was sixteen and going through a phase,' she replied dismissively.

'But now you're twenty-six and now you have fantastic cheekbones, lip-glossed lips—' his eyes lingered on her full mouth for a moment, then fell to the pout of her breasts, travelled lower to her hips and down the length of her legs '—and a dream of a body. My car's outside.'

'Excuse me?' she said, bemused by the sudden veer.

'If you leave the trolley here, I'll take your luggage,' Jader said, and, swinging her travel bag onto one broad shoulder, he picked up her suitcase. 'You reckon you've packed enough to last you the week?' he asked drily, for her suitcase bulged and was heavy.

Ellen hesitated. Should she tell him how she would be extending her stay? No, she had only just arrived, so the news could wait for later.

'Mmm,' she mumbled vaguely. 'I had a great flight,' she said as they set off towards the exit, 'and I managed to catch a glimpse of the statue of Christ the Redeemer before the plane came in to land.' Ellen smiled, recalling the sight of the hundred-and-thirty-foot statue set on a hilltop with arms spread wide. A sight which had brought a catch to her throat, and thrilled her. 'It was breathtaking. As the view of the city—with the mountains, the sea, the offshore islands—was breathtaking,' she chattered on, and her steps quickened. She was needing to hurry in order to keep pace with his long strides.

'I've always longed to visit Rio and particularly at Carnival time, so thank you for asking me over and thanks for providing the air ticket. It was very generous. I've never travelled first class before and—'

'No?' he cut in, sounding surprised.

'No, and being so pampered was terrific.'

'Glad you enjoyed the experience,' Jader said, and directed her out of the airport terminal and along a service road, where vehicles were parked in chaotic disarray. They passed sleek limousines, ramshackle pick-up trucks, a swarm of bright yellow Volkswagen Beetles which, it was evident, did duty as taxis, and eventually reached a gleaming scarlet convertible with a black soft-top roof. 'Here we are.'

As he unlocked the boot and started to fit her bags inside, Ellen stretched up her arms. Back in London the February weather had been chill and wet, but here a golden sun shone in a crystalline blue sky.

'It's warm already,' she said, luxuriating in the caress of the balmy air on her bare skin.

'A perfect day for the beach,' Jader remarked.

Ellen looked down at where he was arranging her luggage, the slate-grey cloth of his jacket pulled taut across his shoulders as he heaved and stretched.

'But you're going to work?' she hazarded.

'I am.' Jader slammed the boot lid shut and straightened. 'I have a business meeting which it's vital I attend, so I'm afraid I'll have to drop you off and leave you until the evening.'

'That's OK,' Ellen assured him. 'I'm happy to go around on my own; I don't need a chaperon. I'm a grown woman now.'

His eyes dipped appreciatively to her body. 'So I see,' he murmured.

Swivelling, Ellen walked around to the passenger door. When making her statement she had unconsciously squared her shoulders, which had emphasised the high curve of her breasts—and drawn his attention. Did Jader believe she had done it deliberately, as a kind of look-at-me come-on? Perhaps. But just as she would never sidle up to a strange man—no matter how appealing he might be—neither did she act the flirt. Whilst she would not criticise such behaviour in others, it went against her personal code of conduct. Ellen pressed her hand down on the doorhandle. Yet his look had created a flutter of satisfaction inside her. A sensual satisfaction.

'I shall also be busy tomorrow and on Friday,' Jader continued as he eased his long body into the car, 'but after that I'm free. The office shuts down for Carnival.'

Ellen settled herself in the seat beside him. She had not noticed the make, but the convertible was style on wheels—smooth, rolling body lines, magnolia leather upholstery, a polished mahogany dashboard which included a built-in telephone and on-board computer. Reaching back, she positioned her bulky camera bag safely on the rear seat. The car was also unusually roomy.

'I'd always thought the Moreira offices were in São Paulo,' she reflected as she fixed the buckle of her seat belt.

'Our main offices, the headquarters of the Moreira Iron Ore Company, are.' Jader paused, frowning. 'However, several years ago my father set up a different business operation on the outskirts of Rio and it's problems with that which I'm having to deal with. For months now I've been spending a minimum of two days a week up here.'

At the mention of his father, Ellen had frowned. 'I was so sorry to receive your letter telling me that Conrado had died,' she said. 'It must've been a dreadful shock.'

'It was,' he acknowledged, his expression suddenly bleak. Sliding a hand inside his jacket, Jader took a pair of gold-rimmed sunglasses from his waistcoat pocket and put them on. 'Conrado was only sixty and appeared to be in excellent health,' he said as he turned the key in the ignition. 'Then the coronary struck and, within minutes, it was all over.'

'I'm sorry,' she said again, and without warning her blue eyes were swimming with tears. 'He was a lovely person.' She swallowed. 'I was very fond of him.'

In order to ease out around two other vehicles at what seemed an impossible angle, Jader looked back away from her over his shoulder. 'Is that right?' he said.

A line cut between her brows. His voice was clipped and the question had sounded sarcastic, barbed—as if he did not believe her. Ellen gave herself a mental shake. No, she was unused to his inflection and must be reading him wrong. The query had been benign.

'It is; I cared about your father. When did the coronary happen?' she went on.

Jader slid into first gear and, with a purring growl of the engine, the convertible sprang away like a powerful metallic panther.

'Last September,' he said.

'September?' Ellen echoed, in surprise.

Because he had written to her just a fortnight ago, she had assumed that his father's death had occurred a few weeks earlier.

Jader nodded. 'You've informed Vivienne?' he enquired.

'I have, and she asked me to give you her deepest sympathy.'

'Thank you. How is she?'

'My mother is well.' Ellen hesitated, aware of stepping onto what could be delicate ground. 'I mentioned on the phone that she lives in France now. Well, three years back she got married again. To Bernard. He's French and they live in his château near Toulouse.'

'Is Vivienne deliriously happy?' Jader enquired.

Again his voice sounded clipped and sarcastic, but when she swung him a look the tinted lenses obscured any expression in his eyes.

'She's content,' Ellen replied carefully.

'But it's not a once-in-a-lifetime, made-in-heaven love?'

'No, though she and Bernard have been friends for many years and their relationship will last. Come what may,' she insisted, feeling thrust onto the defensive.

'Lucky them,' Jader remarked.

Ellen frowned. His clipped manner had not been her imagination. Jader was irritated and a vaguely communicated sense of disapproval lurked below the surface. Might he have a hang-up about a certain truth from the past? she wondered. Her teeth dug into her lower lip. A truth which had once had *her* hung up for years.

No; she was being overly sensitive. Whilst what Conrado would have told him must have shocked, Jader had had ample time to recover. And he was a man of the world. Besides—the crunch—he would never have invited her to spend a holiday in Rio unless he had come to terms with it, wanted to bury the hatchet and be friends. She wanted them to be friends, too, Ellen thought. She wanted it *so* much.

Jader's irritation must have sprung from another source. Like what? she wondered. As he overtook a couple of cars, executing a swift gear change and pressing his foot down hard again on the accelerator, Ellen became conscious of the tensing of the strong, grey-trousered thigh which was parallel to hers. Being under pressure at work, Jader doubtless—and understandably—felt a mite irked by the journey out to the airport which had intruded into the start of his day. A journey which could be classed as her fault.

She eyed the increasingly heavy traffic. And the fact that they had hit the morning rush hour and could be taking longer than he had anticipated would not help.

'There's the Sugarloaf Mountain,' Jader said all of a sudden.

Ellen peered out. They had reached a parkway, edged with manicured green lawns and palm trees. To the left, through buildings, were intermittent flashes of a turquoise sea; to the right rose hillsides of white-walled, red-roofed houses, while in the hazy distance she saw a miniature mountain. Slender black threads connected the mountain with a lower mound and, halfway along, sunshine glittered on a tiny cable car.

She grinned. 'One of the things I'd like to do is go up on the—' Becoming aware of a shape creeping stealthily

into the edge of her vision, she glanced sideways. 'Grief!'
she yelped, and made a frantic grab at her seat belt.

Parallel lines of vehicles were hurtling along the parkway, which, so the white markings decreed, was two-lane.
Yet only in theory, for a decrepit taxi driven by a cool-
dude character in a back-to-front baseball cap and green
mirror sunglasses had squeezed in between the convertible
and an adjacent Mercedes. There were mere inches to
spare—between them and the taxi, between them and the
grassy bank. Ellen sat rigid. Only her chauffeur's firm grip
on the wheel and steel nerves were preventing a collision.

Throwing up a hand, which struck her as insanely cav-
alier, Jader gesticulated his expressive disgust at the ma-
noeuvre, but when the culprit ignored him he grinned.

'Now you know why Brazil produces so many top-class
racing drivers,' he said.

'And now I understand why Brazil has one-hundred-car
pile-ups,' Ellen responded, recalling an incident which his
father had once told her about. She hardly dared breathe.
Samba music was blaring through the taxi's open windows
and—oh, no!—the driver had begun jerking his shoulders
around in time to the beat. 'But I didn't fly all this way in
order to perish in a mock Grand Prix before—' she was
trying to be jokey, but her voice quavered '—I've even
unpacked.'

Jader reached for her hand. 'There's no need to be
frightened, *querida*,' he said, and, raising her fingers to his
lips, he kissed them.

In an instant, Ellen's fear was eclipsed by a heart-
thudding awareness of *him*. Of the touch of his mouth on
her skin, of the clasp of his long, golden-skinned fingers
around her paler ones, of his smouldering brown eyes.

She withdrew her fingers. 'I'd rather you kept two hands
on the wheel,' she told him shakily.

Jader laughed. 'Yes, ma'am,' he replied, and obeyed.

A moment later, the taxi dropped back.

Ellen linked her hands tight in her lap. Calm down, she told herself. You're overreacting. Even if Jader had called her '*querida*', which she knew translated as 'darling', his kiss had been the charming yet casual gesture of the Brazilian male. It meant nothing. Nevertheless, that initial sexual attraction remained alive and kicking. She had seen it flare in the depths of his eyes—and felt her response in the tightening ache of her breasts. An ache which had filled her with a sudden and violent longing to make love.

Ellen's brow furled. She did not usually fall victim to such acute need, so was jet lag playing strange games with her hormones? Or as she had picked Jader unerringly out of the airport crowd could he have unerringly homed in on a peculiar vulnerability in her? She felt a twinge of alarm. The latter seemed more credible.

'You want to go on the cable car while you're here, and what else would you like to do?' he enquired.

'Travel up Corcovado to see the Christ statue near to,' Ellen replied, grateful for the matter-of-fact conversation, 'and visit all the famous beaches, and—'

As she reeled off a list of places which she had selected from the guide books, Jader gave her more information about them and went on to suggest other sightseeing ideas.

'I don't suppose your father ever married again?' Ellen said, when their discussion of her proposed itinerary came to an end.

The query was hesitant. She did not wish to dig too deeply into the past and unearth awkward skeletons, but after a decade without any communication there was a gap in her knowledge which she needed to fill.

Jader frowned against the sunshine. 'As a matter of fact, he did,' he replied.

Ellen's face broke into a delighted smile. 'That's wonderful! I'm so pleased.' She hesitated, her expression becoming sombrely enquiring. 'Did Conrado and his wife manage to have much time together before he died?'

'They had over nine years.'

Her head whipped round and she stared at his profile. 'Nine years?' she repeated.

'Conrado remarried a few months after his relationship with your mother—' Jader halted, as if needing to select a suitable phrase '—was terminated,' he settled on.

'Oh. I hoped he'd find a new love, but I didn't really think that he would and I certainly never imagined it would happen so quickly.' Ellen was silent and pensive for a few moments. 'What is his wife—his widow—like?' she asked curiously.

'Yolanda's Brazilian, brunette. She was much younger than Conrado—and very different to Vivienne.'

What did that mean? Ellen wondered. A sharpness had entered his tone, so did Jader feel a lingering antagonism towards her mother? Given the circumstances, it was always possible.

'But now Conrado's dead,' she said sadly. She thought of how friendly and reliable and genuine the older man had been, and of the bond which had formed between them. A close, loving bond which she had treasured. 'His wife must be heartbroken,' Ellen said, imagining how the woman would have adored him—and recalling how painful it had been when Conrado had disappeared from her own life.

Jader swung off the parkway and onto a road which snaked beneath soaring stone cliffs and into the densely built sprawl of the city. 'Yolanda's greatest worry is the kids,' he said.

'Your father had more children?'

'Three.' His expression had been stern, but now his eyes crinkled at the corners and his mouth softened into a smile. 'Luiz, who's coming up to nine, and two little girls, Julia and Natalya, who are seven and six.'

Ellen raised her brows. The surprises were coming thick and fast, and yet this latest news ought not to surprise because she had known how Conrado, a widower, had always hoped that one day he might extend his family beyond Jader, a much loved only child.

'They're young to have lost their father,' she sympathised. 'My father died when I was a baby—'

'That long ago?' Jader cut in. 'I didn't realise.'

'When I was a year old, so I have no memory of him. I wish I had,' she said wistfully, and looked out at the road ahead.

The rush hour resembled the chaos theory with horse-power. Red lights were continually jumped, lanes repeatedly switched, carelessly parked vehicles caused a perpetual hazard, and yet, amazingly, the traffic kept moving.

'Are you married?' Ellen asked as they drove along.

OK, he might feel a certain lust for her and—she glanced at the blunt-tipped fingers which controlled the wheel—he wore no ring, but that did not preclude his having a wife. And children. Indeed, his looks, sex appeal and wealth combined to make Jader de Sa Moreira a highly desirable male package and he had probably been snatched up long ago.

'No,' he replied.

'Do you live with someone?'

'Not now, though I have done.' Jader gave an easy, very masculine smile. 'And I've had lovers of the live-out variety.'

'Lots, I would imagine,' Ellen said, a mite tartly.

'You imagine wrong. I'm not promiscuous,' he said,

sounding abruptly offended. He swung her a look. 'However, I am thirty-five years old and it is red blood which flows through my veins.'

'What you mean is long-term commitment doesn't appeal, but affairs do.'

'What I mean is I haven't met the right woman,' Jader countered.

Ellen raised her eyes. 'Spare me the cliché!'

'It's true,' he said mildly.

'And who, may I ask, is "the right woman"?'

Jader thought for a moment. 'Someone bright and sexy, who's strong enough to stand up to me. A woman who has her own thing going, because I wouldn't want someone living through me. And she must be unquestionably faithful, as I'd be faithful to her. But for now—' he moved his shoulders '—I'm adult and single, and if I enjoy sex—responsible sex with a willing partner—is that a crime? People are so often schizophrenic on the subject. They love sex and yet they have all kinds of guilt feelings about it.' His lips stretched into a slow smile. 'People like you.'

'Me?' Ellen protested indignantly.

'We wouldn't be having this conversation if you weren't a strait-laced Anglo-Saxon with a buttoned-up attitude.'

She frowned. Her friends and colleagues at work often teased her about the rip-roaring love life she could have if only she took the opportunities which came her way, and it was annoying to discover that Jader had also tagged her with the 'prim and proper' label. Ellen plucked tetchily at a loose thread on the knee of her jeans. She had her full quota of physical desires and sexual needs, but she was a touch more circumspect than most, that was all.

'Where are we?' she asked, in a deliberate and somewhat desperate diversionary tactic.

After driving through city streets where fifties-style office blocks competed for space with ancient churches and modern shopping malls, they had reached a T-junction and straight ahead lay the shimmering sea.

Jader swung right. 'Copacabana,' he said.

Excitement surged inside her. Ellen had wondered whether, as famous places sometimes do, Copacabana might disappoint, but the arc of shore which curved for two or three miles into the distance was magical. On the land side of the road, which a sign declared was the Avenida Atlantica, there were pavement cafés, bars, ritzy shops and hotels, backed by towering, glistening skyscrapers. While towards the ocean a broad pavement tiled in exotic black and white mosaics gave onto a vast expanse of pearly sand.

It had yet to reach nine a.m., but already beach life was in full swing. Joggers pounded to and fro, youths played energetic volleyball, briefly clad sunbathers stroked on tanning lotion. An intermingling of races had produced bodies of ebony and teak, through *café au lait* to white, and, thanks to Rio's almost fanatical exercise cult, most of the bodies were beautiful. Ellen grinned. The beach was a poseur's paradise, the strutting strides and sway of hips announcing loud and clear that the beautiful people expected to be looked at.

'There's a saying that in São Paulo the *paulistas* work and pay taxes, while in Rio the *cariocas* dance samba and go to the beach,' Jader told her.

She laughed. 'And here's proof. Getting myself organised at such short notice took an effort,' Ellen continued, her eyes swinging from side to side as she eagerly drank in the sights, 'but thank you again for making it possible for me to have a holiday here.'

'It's Conrado whom you should really thank,' he said.

'Conrado?' she queried.

Jader slowed to allow two old men in bathing trunks and carrying fold-up canvas chairs to cross the road in front of them. 'When I was going through his papers after he died, I found a letter he'd written to me in which he said he knew how you'd dreamed of seeing Rio and that you might enjoy a visit.'

Ellen's brow puckered. 'So when you got in touch you were obeying his instructions.'

'I was picking up on Conrado's suggestion,' Jader responded.

She gazed out at the beach again, though now she did not see it. To be told that Jader had invited her out of a sense of filial duty altered everything. It kicked the legs out from under her cherished reconciliation theory. It put a different slant on his irritation and meant that she should rethink the subliminal disapproval which she had been so eager to explain. It switched her from a red-carpet guest to a second-class citizen, one who was here on sufferance.

Ellen's temper began to spark. She felt demeaned and betrayed—and cross. Though if she had not been cross there was a chance she could have wept.

'But it was Conrado who instructed—my mistake, *suggested*,' Ellen adjusted astringently, 'that you should send me a first-class air ticket and—' she glanced out to find that they were passing the Copacabana Palace Hotel, which was a huge white birthday cake of a building '—no doubt arrange for me to stay in a five-star hotel.' She dispensed a razor of a smile. 'Perhaps he also pinned a wad of reals to his letter to enable you to pay for my vacation?'

Whisking off his tinted glasses, Jader fixed her with a flint-edged gaze. 'The first-class travel was my idea and I'm financing everything,' he said, 'personally.' The glasses were snapped closed and he thrust them back into his waistcoat pocket.

'However, you're not staying in a hotel, you're staying with me.'

'With you?' Ellen protested, and heard herself squeak. She brought down the level of her voice. 'Where with you?' she demanded.

'At the apartment which I'm renting in Rio. There are two bedrooms and ample space.'

'But—'

'When I rang to confirm flight times you mentioned being much involved in your career, so I assume you don't have a husband who might raise objections. And I doubt you have a live-in lover.' Jader arched a sardonic brow. 'Heaven forbid.'

'Neither,' Ellen told him.

'Have you ever had a live-in lover?'

'No,' she said, aware that she could be regarded as being out of sync with the times.

'Surprise, surprise,' Jader remarked drily. 'How about a boyfriend?'

'Not at the moment,' Ellen replied, and promptly cursed herself. She could have lied; she *should* have lied and laid claim to some hot amorous liaison—or two, or three—but instead she appeared to be confirming his image of her as the prim and proper Miss Blanchard. 'I'm not a virgin,' she added impetuously.

'Alleluia,' he drawled.

Her cheeks burned bright pink. What on earth had made her say that? She did not need to prove anything to him, so why was she sharing such personal and private information?

'Even so, I don't imagine you've had lots of lovers,'

Jader said, smiling devilishly as he reworked the comment she had made to him earlier.

'Two,' she said, and straight away wondered why she had provided the number. 'I'm sure your apartment is comfortable,' Ellen hurried on, fearful of blurting out yet more confidences, 'and the offer is kind, but—'

'You think I'm Vlad the Impaler?' he demanded, suddenly losing his patience.

'No, no.'

She did not regard him as a threat; what bothered her was the sexual vulnerability which he appeared to have exposed within her and which, if they were together too much, she had a nasty suspicion might prove troublesome. If only she did have a man in her life, Ellen thought; then her emotions would not be so capricious and her defences would not have seemed so alarmingly fragile.

She braced herself to protest again. 'I'm sure—'

'Look, it's Carnival week and every damned hotel is full,' Jader rasped.

'Every hotel? You've tried them all?'

'My secretary has. She's tried every place which is halfway decent.'

Ellen bristled. Whilst she did not want to stay with him, it was riling to discover that he had been equally keen to find her alternative accommodation.

'Then perhaps you should've issued your invitation earlier?' she suggested tautly. 'If you found the letter after Conrado died, you've had several months but instead you left it to the last minute. I wonder why?' Her look dripped acid. 'Could it be because getting in touch just two weeks ago vastly reduced the likelihood of me being able to make the trip? Because you hoped I'd need to say thanks, but no, thanks, and let you off the hook?'

A nerve pulsed in his temple. 'I'm sure that on mature

reflection,' Jader said heavily, 'you'll see that if I hadn't been agreeable to you sampling the delights of Rio I need not have invited you. After all, you didn't know my father had died, nor were you aware of the letter containing his—' he paused to insert a terse emphasis '—*suggestion*. And if I hadn't told you you would never've known.

'As to your last-minute theory, why not try another? You may recall my saying how I've spent the last few months commuting between São Paulo and Rio. I've been overseeing two businesses and working near enough fourteen hours a day, which has left very little time for me to get my mind around to other matters. Yes, I should've contacted you earlier,' he acknowledged, 'but time flies.'

Ellen scowled. She did not appreciate being sidelined as 'other matters', yet she was forced to admit that his explanation had credibility. Some. She was not wholly convinced, but she would give him the benefit of the doubt. For now.

'Even so, you would never have issued the invitation if it hadn't been for Conrado,' she said, her hurt making her sharply accusing. 'And now,' Ellen continued, 'after scouring Rio for that elusive vacant hotel room, you're stuck with me?' She flashed a plastic smile. 'Poor you.'

'I'll survive.' Jader's brown eyes swung from the road to travel down her body. 'After all, there have to be worse things for a man who's been working and not playing for heaven knows how long than sharing his living space with a young, pretty and highly watchable blonde,' he said silkily.

Ellen's hands curled into fists. The arch of his brow had made it brutally plain that when Jader had looked at her he'd been mentally stripping away every stitch of her clothing and imagining what she looked like naked. But what was even more infuriating was the fact that she had

found his look arousing! A frisson had shivered her skin
and she had felt heart-bangingly aware of them as male
and female.

'I won't be around too much,' she declared defiantly.
'I'm a photo-journalist—'

'Which explains the fancy gear,' Jader broke in, jerking
his head back towards her camera bag.

'Correct—and while I'm here I shall be taking a photographic record of the city, in order to illustrate a number
of articles which I plan to write.'

He frowned. 'This is why you were so keen to come?'

Ellen looked out at a beachfront stall which was fes-
tooned with yellow and green Brazilian football strip
T-shirts. Although visiting Rio had been a long-time am-
bition, and whilst it had put a most useful career opportunity on her agenda, the impetus for making the journey—
the essential delight—had been her belief that the invitation signalled Jader's desire to forgive and forget and, at
long last, draw a line under the past. But she had miscal-
culated.

She bobbed her head. 'Absolutely,' she declared.

'Who do you work for?' he asked.

'For the past three years, I've been with The Reporter
newspaper group—'

Jader lifted his brows. 'You must be good.'

'I try. It was an interesting job which took me all over
the UK and to different European countries, but I left at
the end of last month because I want to go freelance.
Which is how I was able to make this trip at such short
notice.' Ellen swung him a pert glance. 'You asked me at
precisely the right time—or the wrong time—whichever
way you might care to look at it. I shall have to work from
home at first,' she continued, 'but as soon as I can I intend
to open an office. However, that's going to take money—'

'How much?' he cut in.

'After doing my sums, I reckon that to rent premises in a suitable location, employ a part-time secretary, and equip a darkroom, I need thirty thousand pounds. I have some savings and I should be able to sell articles about Rio to several papers and magazines, so that'll get me off to a good start. I'd like to photograph the Carnival parade—'

'I have tickets,' Jader told her.

'Excellent!' Ellen enthused, then paused. 'Did your father suggest in his letter that you should buy tickets?' she asked suspiciously.

A muscle tightened in his jaw. 'No, I thought it up all on my own,' he grated. 'And as tickets are grabbed up months in advance it took some greasing of palms. I also thought you might find it fun to attend a fancy-dress ball,' he went on, 'and, as long as it suits, we'll be going to one on Saturday.'

'It does suit and thank you.' Ellen's brow crinkled. 'Is Conrado's wife aware that I'm here?' she asked. 'And, if so, what did she think about his suggestion?'

'Yolanda isn't aware of your visit and I didn't show her the letter. It seemed more diplomatic to keep it to myself.'

'She doesn't know about my mother?' Ellen queried.

Jader swung left, heading away from the beach and along a street lined with stylish shops, art galleries and restaurants.

'She knows of her existence. Conrado told me that one evening when he'd had a little too much to drink he made some reference to his friendship with Vivienne, but the next day he said she was just someone he'd known on a business basis.'

'He didn't want his wife to realise they'd had an affair?'

Jader shook his head. 'He felt she mightn't like it— though he wasn't entirely sure whether she believed the business acquaintance claim. Yolanda lives in Rio, but there's no chance of us accidentally running into her,' he carried on, 'because, like half the population, she prefers to leave town at Carnival time. She's taken the children to Campos do Jordão, which is a pretty little place in the mountains which has an air of Switzerland about it. Her family's had a chalet there for years and the kids love it.'

'If I hadn't been coming, would you have gone home to São Paulo?' Ellen enquired.

He nodded. 'Yes.'

'Then thank you for remaining in Rio,' she said, a touch stiffly, 'and thank you for your hospitality.'

'My pleasure. We're travelling parallel to Ipanema beach which is a few blocks away to the left,' Jader explained. 'And that—' they were driving down a shady, tree-lined avenue and he indicated the diamond sparkle of sunlit water ahead '—is the Lagoa Rodrigo de Freitas, the lagoon. The apartment which I'm leasing overlooks it.'

Ringed by a road, grassy verge and, nearer to the water, a walking-cum-cycle track, the lagoon stretched out, blue and tranquil.

'Is it a natural lake?' Ellen asked.

'Yes, I understand it used to be part of a sixteenth-century sugar plantation. On the far side, if you look below the mountains, there's a racecourse, the Botanical Gardens and a funfair,' Jader continued.

Ellen had just picked out a distant Ferris wheel, when he swung into the courtyard of an apartment block. There was a glimpse of a pillared portico, of purple bougainvillea tumbling over white balconies, then the convertible dipped down into the underground car park.

Jader lived on the sixth, and top, floor of the building. They went up in a lift which opened onto a small private vestibule, where he unlocked a studded oak door. Standing aside, he ushered her ahead of him into a marble-floored entrance hall.

'Cloakroom, kitchen, my room,' Jader said, indicating doors in quick succession. He nudged his shoulder against a door which swung into a bedroom decorated in chic apricot and white—white carpet, a luscious apricot satin bedspread, white louvred dressing table and wardrobes. 'This is your room, with bathroom.' Setting down her luggage, he shepherded her back out into the hall. 'Before you unpack and before I leave, there's something I have to tell you.'

His manner brisk, he directed her up a few steps which flowed gracefully from the hall and into a spacious living room. Ellen looked around. Sunlight streamed across a wide terrace and in through French windows hung with dusky pink silk curtains. A pink and pale green striped sofa sat on one of several cream rugs which covered the marble floor and there were two matching armchairs and a leather-topped coffee-table. Oil paintings of colonial Rio were pinned four-square on one wall, while a bureau stood against another. Although it had the somewhat sparse look of rented accommodation, the room was attractive.

Gesturing for her to be seated on the sofa, Jader sat down opposite in an armchair. He shot a snowy-white cuff and straightened the knot of his maroon silk tie.

'Conrado also left you some shares,' he said.

Ellen's eyes flew open wide. 'Shares?' she repeated, in astonishment. 'Shares in what?'

'In the company he set up in Rio, which manufactures cars. He's left you ten per cent. Now the shares as—'

'What kind of cars are they?' she asked.

'You've just been in one.'

'The convertible?' Ellen said wonderingly.

Jader nodded. 'Obviously the shares, as shares, aren't of

any interest to you,' he continued, 'whereas their value is. And they're worth near enough fifty thousand pounds.'

She gave a startled laugh. 'Wow!'

'Sorting out the legalities of my father's estate took time, but now all it needs is for you to sign a bill of sale and for your signature to be witnessed—'

'Who would I be selling the shares to?' Ellen interrupted.

'Me. Conrado left me the other ninety per cent,' Jader said, and pushed back his cuff to inspect the heavy stainless-steel watch which was strapped to his broad wrist. He frowned. Time, it seemed, was now in preciously short supply. 'So when I come back from the office this evening I'll bring a couple of people with me to witness—'

'Don't bother,' she said.

'Excuse me?'

'I'm not sure whether or not I want to sell the shares,' Ellen told him.

CHAPTER TWO

JADER sat forward. 'Not sure? Not sell the shares?' he repeated, as if she had suddenly gone insane. 'But fifty thousand pounds would enable you to set up an office and leave ample cash to spare for new photographic equipment, holidays, a rainy day—' he threw out a hand '—whatever.'

'I'm aware of that,' Ellen said.

'One of the people I'll bring back this evening is the company accountant and he'll verify that you're receiving the full and proper payment.' His eyes darkened. 'I'm not attempting to swindle you,' he said curtly.

'The idea never crossed my mind,' she told him.

'But you think that if you hang onto the shares they could rise in value?' Jader gave a cryptic laugh. 'Sorry, it ain't going to happen. Earlier I mentioned that I was dealing with problems—well, the company's never done more than break even and the increasing cost of materials means that during this coming year it's destined to fall into loss. For months now I've been identifying economies and attempting to find some way of turning the business around, but unless there's a dramatic increase in sales it's impossible. And sales remain—' he slashed a horizontal line through the air '—dead level. Which means that if you keep the shares their worth can only diminish.'

'Maybe,' Ellen said. 'However, before I sign on the dotted line there are some questions which I'd like to ask.'

Jader checked his watch again. Frowned again. 'Questions about what?' he enquired.

'About the functioning of the company.'

'Come on,' he said impatiently. 'That's of no interest to you.'

'I want to know,' Ellen said.

His jaw tightened. 'Do you have to be so bloody-minded?' he demanded.

'Must you steamroller me?' she parried. 'You have a meeting to attend, but don't worry, I shan't take up any more of your time. I'm willing to leave my questions until you return this evening.' Ellen shone him a sugary smile. '*Without* the witnesses.'

Jader hesitated for a moment, then rose to his feet. 'Your wish is my command,' he said, with a polite bow of his head, but his eyes gave him away—they burned with fury. Reaching down, he picked up two keys from the table. 'These are for you. The larger one opens the outer front door of the apartments and the smaller one is for here.'

'Thank you,' she said as he handed them to her.

'I asked the maid to stock up on groceries,' Jader went on, 'so you'll find food in the kitchen for breakfast, if you want it, and for lunch.'

'Cyanide and broken glass?' Ellen enquired.

A faint smile touched his lips. 'I suspect the supermarket could've been out of stock.'

'What bad management. Is the maid coming in today?' she asked, going with him across the living room and down the steps into the hall.

'No. I've given her a couple of weeks off for Carnival. Should you fancy a look at the beach, if you turn left outside the front gate and keep on walking you'll hit Impanema in roughly twenty minutes,' Jader continued, becoming the informative host. 'Alternatively, it's a pleasant stroll beside the lagoon. However, although the education of the street kids means there's been a marked drop in theft recently, like any big city Rio has its dangers; so when you're walking alone don't wear jewellery or take much money,' he warned. 'And hang on tight to your camera.'

'Will do, but I shan't go exploring this morning. I shall unpack and fall into bed.'

'You didn't sleep on the plane?' he asked.

'Not much.' Ellen hooked a tendril of pale hair behind her ear. 'And all of a sudden I feel worn out.'

Jader looked down at her. 'I apologise,' he said. 'I should've realised you'd be tired and left the business about the shares for later.' The crooked, fetching smile bloomed in the corner of his mouth. 'Will you forgive me?'

After berating her, he had switched to placating her—and the persuasion in his smile and the upward tilt of his dark brows was close to irresistible. Ellen gazed coolly back. At sixteen he would have reeled her in like a yo-yo, but now she was older, wiser and far more resilient.

'Perhaps,' she said. 'In time.'

Jader placed his hands on her shoulders. 'Now,' he murmured, and he bent his head and kissed her.

His lips were soft and warm against hers. The clean scent of his skin filled her nostrils. There was an awareness of the lean length of his body, not quite touching hers yet so near. Drugged by his proximity, Ellen swayed closer. Mouth parted on mouth and as the moistness of his tongue grazed hers an electric charge streaked through her. She was sinking into a pool of helpless pleasure when, as unexpectedly as it had begun, the kiss broke and Jader stepped back.

'Sleep well,' he said, his expression unreadable, and his

footsteps rapped out a brisk staccato on the marble floor and, a moment later, the door clicked shut behind him.

Bemused, Ellen pressed the back of her hand to her mouth; her tingling mouth. She had thought she was made of sterner stuff than her sixteen-year-old self, so why had she stood there like a dummy when Jader had kissed her *and* swayed closer? How could she have been so pliable? What had happened to wisdom? She had known that, like his smile, his kiss was a deliberate manipulative ploy. It had been obvious he was attempting to soften her up and seduce her into selling him her shares—soonest!—yet she had fallen for it.

As Ellen walked through to her bedroom, she frowned. But had the embrace been deliberate? she wondered. Was she sure? No, in retrospect his abrupt withdrawal and speedy exit suggested that Jader had kissed her spontaneously—though soon regretted it. Just as he had homed in on a vulnerability in her, so he also seemed to be vulnerable *to* her. She chewed at her lip. Did this make her feel triumphant...or wary? Might mutual vulnerability spell danger?

Ellen sank down on the side of the bed. When flying through the night she had painted a scenario where, with the conflict of the past seemingly resolved, all was sweetness and light between them. She had imagined they would be easy with each other, but the sexual chemistry which fizzed between them eliminated easiness. It disturbed; as did Jader's underlying disapproval. Though why should he disapprove of her *now*? He might have considered her to be the villain of the piece once upon a time, but he must have recognised long ago that not only had she acted from the best motives, but that she had been *forced* to act.

Ellen heeled off one blue denim espadrille and then the other. She would sleep first and unpack later. Jader also had to acknowledge that if anyone should be censured it was her mother.

The pink T-shirt was tugged from her jeans and drawn off over her head. But perhaps her host was dumping his disapproval of Vivienne onto her? Because she happened to be here and available, she was expected to take the flak? Ellen frowned. Whilst she did not know Jader well, she would not have thought him so unfair and yet, though he might not be able to engage her in hand-to-hand combat, she had a feeling that in coming to Rio she had placed herself behind enemy lines. Her eyes shadowed. For him to be so mean-spirited as to bear a grudge against her mother for ten long years seemed out of character too.

Reaching behind her back, Ellen unhooked her bra. She saw no point in dwelling negatively on the past, but if he chose to do so that was his problem. She refused to get uptight.

Shucking off the remainder of her clothes, Ellen climbed into bed. Jader considered she was being contrary in not immediately agreeing to sell him her shares, she mused, and he was right. Her insistence on asking questions about the company had been a perverse delaying tactic, pure and simple. Ellen grinned mischievously, recalling his chagrin. And it had worked.

But she had been annoyed that he should nonetheless take her compliance so much for granted and now—her grin faded—now she was damned if she would rush to oblige a man who, when he had deigned to issue his last-minute invite, had been propelled into it by his father *and* who seemed to be conducting an unjust personal vendetta against her.

Ellen drew the sheet up to her chin. It had been thoughtful of Conrado to suggest that she should visit Rio and generous of him to gift her the shares. Though she understood why, she brooded as her mind travelled back down the years...

Conrado de Sa Moreira had come into her life one summer evening when he had collected her mother from their London apartment. A table had been reserved for dinner for two at a stylish restaurant and instead of buzzing up on the intercom to announce his arrival—whereupon Vivienne would have gone down to the lobby to meet him—an incoming resident had let him into the Victorian mansion block and he had taken the lift to the third floor and rung their bell. It was Ellen who had opened the door.

'You want your money,' she had begun to say, but, instead of the pimply, bucket-toting youth she had expected, had found herself addressing a tall, distinguished-looking man in a smart suit and with dark hair silvered at the temples. 'Sorry, I thought you were the window-cleaner.'

'An easy error to make,' the man had replied, his brown eyes twinkling, 'but my name is Conrado.'

'You're early,' her mother had called, looking out from her bedroom. 'I didn't think Brazilians understood the meaning of early.'

'Almost never,' Conrado had replied, laughing. 'But I couldn't wait to see you.'

Ellen had rolled her eyes. Yet another member of the Vivienne Blanchard fan club, she had thought drily. At an early age, she had realised that her mother was not pretty in the homely, unobtrusive way of other children's mothers—she was importantly beautiful. Vivienne had exquisitely refined features, violet-blue eyes and, with her blonde hair combed back and coiled into a smooth bun at the nape of her neck, possessed a serene patrician elegance.

'You can't see me yet because I'm not ready,' Vivienne said, and smiled at Ellen. 'Take Conrado through to the living room, Ellie, and get him something to drink.'

This was unusual. At forty, her mother continued to draw admirers like the proverbial moths to a flame, but she kept her social life strictly separate from her home life. It was rare that she talked of her escorts and she never brought anyone home. But as soon as she saw how Vivienne chattered and sparkled and *relaxed* in the Brazilian businessman's company Ellen realised that he was special. This time, for the first time to her knowledge, her mother cared. Truly cared.

She understood why. A gentleman in every sense of the word, Conrado was both interesting and interested. He had time for everyone, including the frumpy teenaged Ellen. After that evening, a routine was established where he always came in for a drink and as Conrado talked with her, listened to her, sometimes offered advice, she began to care for him too.

On that occasion he spent six weeks in London and when his business dealings were complete and he flew back to Brazil their lives seemed woefully flat. But a few months later Conrado visited England again, lit up their lives, and this time Ellen went with him and her mother for a weekend in Cornwall. She treasured that weekend, when they felt like a family.

Over the next twelve months, the businessman made further trips and there were other weekends away. Everything seemed perfect, until the day Conrado rang to let Vivienne know he had arrived in London and to advise that this time, on what was a brief visit, he had brought his son, Jader, with him.

'Conrado would like us all to have dinner together tomorrow evening,' Vivienne reported when she replaced the receiver.

Ellen scowled. Conrado often spoke about his beloved son who had recently joined him in his company, but she resented this golden boy who would change their cosy threesome into a four. When they went out to dinner, Ellen resolved to ignore him as much as possible, but Jader de Sa Moreira proved to be a handsome young man who was as charismatic and friendly as his father. Within minutes, she was smitten and after he spent most of the evening talking to her she was madly, thrillingly in love.

After a third dinner, her mother remarked on how pleased Conrado was that the four of them were getting along so well together.

'It's marvellous,' Ellen agreed, and was floating off into a daydream about Jader, who was the most marvellous part of it all, when a thought suddenly occurred to her. She went cold. 'You don't imagine Conrado might be planning to propose to you?' she asked.

Her mother's brow creased. 'I made it clear to him from the start that I wasn't interested in a serious relationship, but—'

'But Conrado's the kind of man who, when he falls in love, expects to be married. And he's fallen in love with you!'

Her mother laughed. 'Don't sound so horrified, Ellie.'

'But you *can't* marry him,' she protested.

'Perhaps not.'

'There's no "perhaps" about it,' Ellen said.

'I suppose so,' her mother said and sighed. 'When Conrado proposes I shall tell him my devotion to your father's memory means I would never consider marrying anyone else.'

'You think he'll believe that? And if he does, you think he won't try to make you change your mind? Be realistic, Mum,' Ellen implored. 'Conrado's a determined individual and smart. He knows how you feel about him, so if you make an excuse he'll realise it's an excuse and continue

to court you, and the situation'll just get worse and worse.'
She had begun to jabber and she snatched in a breath. 'Or
if you say you've decided you don't want to see him again
he won't believe you and he'll demand to know why.'

'You don't expect me to tell him the truth?' Vivienne
enquired, in alarm.

Ellen frowned. 'What's the alternative? I know it'll be
hard, but it's better he should hear it from you than he
should find out from someone else. And there's always a
risk.'

Now patently distressed, her mother closed her eyes. 'I
can't tell him,' she said.

'Mum, the two of you have been close for over a year,
so you owe Conrado your honesty. It's only fair he should
understand why you're unable to become his wife.'

There was a long, fraught silence.

'You're right,' Vivienne agreed, at last, 'but you must
tell him for me.'

Ellen started to protest. 'Mum, it's not my—'

'He and Jader fly back to Brazil tomorrow night, so tell
Conrado tomorrow. After the two of us have spent one last
evening alone together. When I'm at work at the gallery.
Please, Ellie,' her mother begged, opening violet-blue eyes
which were awash with tears.

That evening, Vivienne asked Conrado if he could come
to the Kensington apartment the next morning—and when
he arrived Ellen was there on her own. In a strained voice
she revealed a truth from her mother's past, at which point
Conrado declared that their relationship must end and departed.

Left alone, Ellen sobbed—with hurt, with sorrow, with
regret. She was disconsolately thinking how good life
could have been, if only, when the intercom buzzed. She
expected it to be her mother saying she had called in to

hear how things had gone and had mislaid her key, but the voice she heard was Jader's.

Ellen's teenage heart leapt. Had he come to commiserate? she wondered as she waited for the lift to arrive at their floor. Was he here to say he understood and to comfort her? Would he wrap his arms around her and hold her tight? Please, please. She needed his sympathy and his support. She *craved* it.

But, seconds later, Jader strode into the apartment and accused her of being a souless little bitch who had cruelly and selfishly wrecked his father's relationship with her mother.

Ellen frowned at the ceiling. That Jader should have blamed her had been an adolescent tragedy. She might have only known him briefly, yet she had worshipped him. It was the first time she had let herself care for a man and even though, in retrospect, her feelings could be recognised as infatuation they had been intense. That Jader might care for her had also had the shine of plausibility—then, though not now, Ellen thought wryly.

On that day, Jader's rage had been so great that it would not have surprised her if he had swept vases from tables, kicked the furniture, rammed holes in doors. His anger would have been almost comical—if she had not had to take the full force of it.

Ellen sighed. She had been bemused, tongue-tied, trapped in an agony of fearfulness where she had been scared of him—though even more frightened of what he might say about her mother. However, it had soon become apparent that her accuser was not in full possession of the facts.

Ellen's frown deepened. She had thought that when Conrado divulged the truth—perhaps later that day, or on the flight home, or when they reached Brazil—Jader would get in touch and apologise for lambasting her. Humbly. Tenderly. For days, weeks, months, she had waited for a phone call or a letter, or even for him to arrive in person, but she had waited in vain. And now, ten years later, when she had been expecting reconciliation or, at the very least, a truce, he remained hostile towards her—because of her mother.

Ellen punched at the pillow. As Jader had said, she had changed—and in more ways than just physically. She was tougher. Her days of being a victim were gone. She was in control of her life and ran things her way. Now she could give as good as she got, which meant, Ellen thought rebelliously, that as Jader had kept her waiting for an apology, so she would keep him waiting before she agreed to sell him the shares. Not waiting for ten years, but for a while—and in the meantime she would make him squirm!

Ellen awoke with a start. Where was she? she wondered, in a moment of disorientation, then she realised that she was in Rio de Janeiro, in Jader's apartment, sleeping off her jet lag. She blinked at the drawn curtains and the sunlight which showed behind them. How long had she been asleep? Her head felt as heavy as if she had been comatose for days, but it had probably been just an hour or two.

Pushing back the covers, Ellen stumbled through to the bathroom. A shower would liven her up. She stood beneath the spray, automatically shampooed, soaped and rinsed—and remained half-asleep. She had dried herself and begun to rub at her hair, when she swallowed. Or tried to. Her throat was parched. She needed a drink. Right away.

Hanging the damp bath sheet back over the rail, she found a smaller dry towel and, still rubbing at her wet blonde tresses, padded across the hall and into the kitchen.

Ellen gazed blearily around. There would be cold drinks in the fridge, but where was the fridge? Equipped with the latest modern appliances—ceramic hob, oven, microwave, dishwasher, *et al.*—the kitchen had honey-coloured work-tops, harvest-patterned tiles and a multitude of smooth pine units. The fridge would be hidden away inside one of them somewhere.

Ellen opened the nearest cupboard. It contained a fine china dinner service. There was what looked like everyday white crockery in the next. Baking bowls filled the shelves of the third. When she had investigated one row of low cupboards without success, she started on the next. The towel was hanging loose in her hand and she was stooping down with her bottom poked up in the air, when she heard the sound of footsteps. Startled, Ellen glanced back over her shoulder to see Jader walking into the doorway.

He stopped dead and grinned. 'Tut-tut,' he said, clicking his tongue. 'Naked in the kitchen? The rulebook for but-toned-up Anglo-Saxons can never sanction that.'

Standing up straight, Ellen grasped each end of the towel and stretched it across her breasts. She turned to him. Now at least the front of her was concealed from his view, she thought, with relief—then realised that the towel barely skimmed her hips. As her cheeks flamed pink, Ellen bent, frantically spread-eagling a hand over the exposed triangle of blonde curls which nestled in the cleft between her thighs.

'Vertical,' Jader said.

She looked blankly up at him. 'What?'

'If you hold the towel vertically rather than horizontally, it'll cover the front of you—all of you,' he explained, as if speaking to a slow-witted child. 'Or, to be accurate, it'll cover the parts which you are so desperate to hide.'

Ellen's pink cheeks burned crimson. 'Oh—yes,' she

said, and made a hasty, fumbled, but far more respectable rearrangement. 'What are you doing here?' she demanded, pinning her fingers tight into the top edge of the towel.

'I missed you,' Jader said drily. 'What the hell do you think I'm doing here? I'm back from work.'

'Already?' Ellen protested.

'It's gone six.'

'Has it?' she said, in surprise. 'I've just woken up and I didn't realise.'

Sliding his hands into his trouser pockets and with his jacket flaring back, Jader rested a shoulder against the doorjamb. 'You appeared to be looking for something,' he said.

'For the fridge. I'm thirsty.'

He nodded towards double doors beneath a worktop which she had not yet tried. 'Freezer's on the left, fridge on the right. There's cola, orange juice, soda, beer, wine. Help yourself.'

'Thank you,' Ellen said, but she did not move. If she went to open the fridge, it would mean turning away from him.

A grin tugged at the corner of his mouth. 'I have seen a bare female backside before,' he told her.

'Not mine,' she returned crisply.

'True, and you're obviously keen that I don't so perhaps you'd like me to get your drink for you?' Jader suggested.

Ellen shone him a stiff smile. 'If you would be so kind.'

'What'll you have?'

'Something soft.' He had walked into the kitchen and around her, and she was needing to swivel in order to remain facing him. 'Um—cola.'

'Alcohol is another taboo?' Jader enquired as he opened the fridge and took out a can.

Ellen glowered. He seemed to be branding her as strait-laced again and, for a moment, she was tempted to fling away the towel like the last of the Seven Veils and perform a dance of wild abandon. Though only for a moment.

'No, it isn't,' she replied, 'but right now I want a drink that's long and cold.' Resolutely holding the towel in place, she loosened some fingers. 'Thanks,' she said as he yanked at the ring-pull and gave her the can.

Clasping it to her chest, Ellen sidled hurriedly past him and into the hall. Being so nearly naked in his presence was making her nerves twang like harp strings, but soon she would be inside her bedroom and behind the closed door.

'Would you care for something stronger later?' Jader enquired, coming after her. 'If you tell me, I can fix it and we can take our drinks out onto the terrace.'

To answer him, Ellen was forced to slow her sideways shuffle. 'Um—white wine would be good.'

'A Chardonnay?'

'Please.'

His eyes trailed over her. 'You have a tan,' he remarked.

'The remains of one,' she agreed, for her skin was the colour of pale honey.

'I noticed that it's all over, so you've been sunbathing nude.' Jader wagged a reproving finger. 'Another violation of the Anglo-Saxon rules.'

'I was on a hotel balcony which couldn't be over-looked,' Ellen told him, restarting her shuffle.

'Where?'

Her retreat had to slow again. 'Cyprus.'

'When?'

'I went there just after Christmas.'

'On holiday?'

'On an assignment. You're enjoying this,' Ellen accused, narrowing her eyes at him.

Jader chuckled. 'Every last minute.'

She glanced back to discover, thankfully, that she was just a couple of yards from her bedroom door. 'Louse!' she declared, and sped hotfoot inside.

Ellen opened her suitcase and found fresh underwear. Why, when she had a decent figure, had she been so desperate to cover herself up? she wondered. Why had she acted like some hysterical Victorian maiden? A loose white cotton shirt was pulled on and she stepped into her jeans. Because she was a prisoner of her inhibitions and perhaps *too* demure? Rummaging in her travel bag, Ellen found her hairdrier. Damn. She had packed in such a rush that she had forgotten to bring a Brazilian-friendly plug.

'I don't suppose you have an adaptor?' she asked, walking back into the kitchen where Jader had selected a bottle of wine from amongst several on a rack.

He shook his head. ''Fraid not.'

Ellen shrugged. 'Ah, well, my hair'll dry in the warm air and I can buy an adaptor tomorrow.'

'Are you a vegetarian?' Jader asked as he uncorked the wine.

'No,' she replied. 'Why?'

'Because there's a *rodizio* nearby—a restaurant which specialises in marinated meats—filet mignon, ham, turkey, chicken, pork—which are grilled or roasted over charcoal. Skewers of the meats are brought to the table and the waiters carve off slices, which are served with salads,' he explained. 'It's a typically Brazilian meal and I thought we could go there for dinner this evening.'

On the point of agreeing, Ellen hesitated. There were dark patches beneath his eyes and the lines from his nose to his mouth were tightly drawn. Jader looked tired.

'You said there was food here so why don't I make us something and we eat in tonight?' she suggested.

'You're happy to do that?' he asked, and she heard relief in his voice.

Ellen nodded. 'I'd like a lazy evening. And,' she added pungently, 'I don't expect you to wine and dine me every night.' She took a step towards the door. 'I'll go and unpack.'

Jader loosened his tie in what registered as a sexy male gesture. 'I'll change.'

Twenty minutes later, Ellen walked across the living room towards the open French windows, but as she reached the threshold she stopped. Out on the terrace, Jader was sprawled in a floral-upholstered rattan chair with his head back, his eyes closed and his long legs stretched out. He had changed into a black T-shirt which defined the firm muscles of his chest, a pair of button-fly jeans and loafers.

Her fingers tightened around the handle of the hairbrush which she carried. In the casual clothes, there was an arresting *physicality* about him. A physicality which made her disturbingly aware of being alone with him in his apartment, of the two of them sleeping tonight in rooms which were so close.

Pulling the brush through her hair, Ellen went outside. The heat of the day had subsided, but the air remained balmy. She stood at the balcony rail. The sun had set, leaving a sky streaked with tropical twilight shades of titian, gold and grey. The colours were echoed below the glassy surface of the lagoon and, as her gaze lifted, she saw that all around the lights of the city were starting to blink on like so many sparkling diamonds. Ellen's gaze stretched further. High in the dusk she could see the statue of Christ, only this time it was bathed in golden light.

'Lovely,' she murmured.

'You are,' a voice said, and she turned to find Jader standing beside her.

Ellen gave a slightly tense smile. No matter how often compliments came her way, she always had a hard time with them. And to find one coming from him was even harder.

Crossing to a low rattan table which sat between the two chairs, Jader picked up a cut-crystal glass of wine in each hand and passed one to her. 'Welcome to Rio,' he said.

Ellen stuck her brush into her hip pocket. 'I look forward to an interesting stay,' she replied lightly, and they touched glasses and drank.

'You wanted to ask questions about the car company,' he reminded her, and they sat down. 'Shoot.'

Retrieving her brush, Ellen wielded it again. If she did not keep brushing every so often, when her hair dried it would be a mass of kinks.

'Although I don't know much about cars,' she began, 'to me the convertible appears to be a quality vehicle.'

'It is,' Jader said, before she could get any further. 'It's as good as, if not better than, all the comparable luxury cars in its class and at its price.'

'So why has the company never done more than break even?'

'Because—' He stopped and started again. 'To begin at the beginning, my father set up the car plant here for two reasons. One—' Jader held up a long finger '—because Yolanda comes from Rio and she didn't want to move. And—'

'Conrado was so considerate of her wishes? That's nice,' Ellen intruded, thinking that, with São Paulo only an hour or so away by air, for him to start a business in Rio in order to please his wife indicated a deep affection. In truth, she had been amazed that Conrado should have fallen for another woman so soon after his affair with her mother, but, she mused, love did not obey rules and could strike at the most unexpected moment. 'He didn't think of giving up work when he got married?' she asked.

'Yes, he did. He tried retirement for a few months, but he became restless.' Jader frowned, then raised a second finger. 'And two, he went into car manufacture because it gave him an entirely new interest. Up until then he'd always been immersed in the iron ore company. It'd been the mainspring of his life, but his attitude changed—' Jader frowned again '—and as the months went by he left more and more of the decisions to me, until I was running the show.'

'You were young to take control of such a large business,' Ellen remarked.

'I guess, and I had my share of sleepless nights,' he said wryly, 'but everything turned out fine.'

'The iron ore company is making a profit?' she asked, thinking that it was difficult to imagine Jader losing sleep over anything.

He smiled. 'We've just had our best year ever... So Conrado set up what you could call a "fun" company,' he continued. 'He did so basically to give himself something to do and because he'd always been a car fanatic. For the first two or three years when the factory was built and the convertible was being designed and prototypes produced he was keen, but his children always came first. He started taking mornings off, days off, and by the time Natalya appeared he was devoting the greater part of his time and energy to them.'

Ellen thought of Conrado with the young wife whom he had loved so much and with the children she had given him. In her mind's eye, she saw the second-time-around father nursing a drooling baby and playing a gentle game of catch with a toddler. They must have been a close-knit and happy family. The kind of family she had always wanted to belong to, she thought whimsically.

'Conrado was content for the company to just rub along?' she said.

Jader nodded. 'He realised he'd be forced to take action sooner or later, but before he could get that far the coronary struck, and—' he took a swig from his glass '—sorting everything out has fallen to me.'

'Does his wife know that Conrado left me the shares?' she enquired.

'Yes. As the bequest formed a part of his will, Yolanda had to know.'

'What was her reaction?' Tilting her head to one side, Ellen brushed through the length of her hair. 'If she believes Vivienne was just a business acquaintance, surely she must think that it's odd?'

'You'd imagine so,' Jader agreed, 'but she's never said anything.'

Ellen's brow furrowed. 'Doesn't she feel that her children ought to have had the shares?'

'Again, Yolanda hasn't commented. But they've each inherited a chunk of the iron ore stock which is held in trusts for them and her family are well off, so they're not going to be paupers.'

'You've inherited iron ore stock too?' she asked.

'The lion's share.' Jader watched the motion of the brush as it swept from the top of her head and down through the silky waterfall of almost dry wheat-blonde hair. For a moment he seemed to be hypnotised, then he roused himself. 'Now,' he said, his determined tone indicating that he was fixing on what he regarded as the vital point of the conversation, 'because you live in England the car company is of no interest and the shares are of no use to you—'

Ellen raised a silencing hand. 'Hold on a minute,' she said. 'If the convertible is so good, why can't you increase the sales? If an advertising campaign was launched, say, offering free servicing for a year or two, or something—'

'We've tried that. Believe me, we've tried everything,' Jader said impatiently. 'The trouble is that the kind of Brazilians who can afford to buy the convertible are the kind of people who prefer to buy an imported European car. It's a status thing. Snob appeal. Street cred. People prefer to spend a darn sight more for what often amounts to a darn sight less, and be seen driving around in a car made in Europe.

'And, although the advertising people have attacked the problem from every angle they can think of, there seems to be no way of getting round it. The factory has the capacity to manufacture four times the number of cars we're currently making, but unless sales increase the company goes belly up within the next couple of years.'

Ellen put down her hairbrush. Like his son, Conrado de Sa Moreira had been intelligent, with an incisive grasp of business, and it seemed odd that, as a first step, he should have failed to apply his analytical skills to the acceptance of the convertible in the local market. She took a sip of white wine. But perhaps he had been so wrapped up in his new bride that he had neglected to give sufficient time to the matter?

'So what do you have in mind for our company?' Ellen enquired.

Jader's head jerked up. *'Our?'* he demanded.

'I am a co-owner. In fact, I probably qualify as a director.' She opened her blue eyes wide. 'Yes?'

'Could be,' he muttered.

'Your plans for our company?' she prodded, when Jader remained silent and frowning.

'At the moment I'm sounding out would-be buyers.'

'Your intention is to sell?'

'Yes, though no one's interested in the business as a going concern. The factory'll have to be dismantled and the assets—plant, land—sold off as and when.' He raked spikes of dark hair back from his brow. 'The last thing I want to do is put people out of work, but—' He sighed.

'Thanks for the information,' Ellen said. 'I'll need to weigh up what you've told me and see if I agree.'

'Agree about the future of the company and whether or not it ceases to trade?' Jader demanded brusquely, his brown eyes blazing. 'That decision is not yours to make.'

'OK, but owning ten per cent of the shares has to give me some rights.' She tilted a brow. 'You have the majority vote, but if you're so keen to acquire my holding then I assume I have to be consulted about such an important decision and others which may occur along the way?'

'You do,' he snapped, looking as if he would dearly like to stand her up against the wall and shoot her. 'Though it's just a procedure and I can overrule you.'

'But it's a procedure you'd prefer to do without,' Ellen said, and grinned. Ten years ago, Jader's anger would have had her quaking in her boots, yet now she was deriving a certain zest from this contest of wills. She might not have the upper hand, but she possessed some power over him and it felt good. 'I'd like to take a tour of the factory while I'm here,' she announced.

A large fist clenched, the knuckles showing white. 'You are giving me the run-around,' Jader rasped.

'*Au contraire*, Pierre. You may see no alternative to closure, but two minds are better than one,' Ellen declared, 'and—who knows?—I could come up with a brainwave which'll kick-start sales into the upward mode and save the day. Then,' she added merrily, 'perhaps I'll pack in photo-journalism and become a working director of the company.'

He muttered something which sounded like the Portuguese equivalent of 'over my dead body'.

'I might be a real asset,' Ellen said.

'And you could be out by just two letters,' Jader retorted. 'But even in this fantasy you'd never be willing to live in Brazil.'

'Why not? I already speak a little of the language; I'm out of practice, but I'm good at languages so—'

'You didn't want to live here ten years ago.'

'That's not true,' Ellen protested, but he ignored her.

'You live in England and you're in Rio for a week. One short *week*,' Jader stressed, 'and then you're boarding a plane and flying home. Which means that—'

'I'm in Rio for a month,' she interrupted.

'A month?' he echoed.

She grinned at his look of horror. 'There's no need to get all bent out of shape; I don't intend to be shacking up with you for the next four weeks. I'll stay here until the Carnival's over and then move into a hotel or maybe a motel. Yes, that'll be cheaper,' Ellen decided. 'I noticed some motels on our way in from the airport, so I shall book into one of those.'

'You can try, but they won't want you after the first twenty-four hours,' he said.

Her brow puckered. 'Why ever not?'

'Because in Rio the motels are not designed for tourists but for lovers.'

'Lovers?' Ellen protested.

'They're Brazil's answer to the permissive society and were originally started to give young couples who live at home until they marry some privacy,' Jader told her. 'Now, however, they're also used by married couples who wish to get away from the kids for an hour or two, and by those conducting extra-marital affairs. The rooms often come with mirrored ceilings and vibrating beds, and at some motels they even provide a mask to wear in the lift so that you won't be recognised.'

She looked at him. A smile was playing around the edges of his mouth, as if he expected Miss Prim and Proper to be shocked.

'So I'll need to find other accommodation,' Ellen said, and added lightly, 'Though if I should become involved in a holiday romance I now know where to go.'

Jader hoisted a brow. 'You'd be open to a holiday romance?' he enquired.

'Why not? It is red blood which flows in my veins,' she declared, quoting his own phrase back at him, 'and Rio is the city of lovers. Perhaps I could come to the factory tomorrow?' she said.

'Sorry, I'm tied up. Though,' he added pungently, 'if you did come, you wouldn't have a clue what you were looking at.'

'You want me to be a sleeping partner?' Ellen demanded, but when he grinned she immediately regretted her choice of phrase.

'We're back to this holiday romance of yours?' Jader drawled. He moved expansive shoulders. 'Well…'

His shrug appeared to signify acceptance and it seemed as if he was suggesting that *they* should have an affair. Ellen's breath caught in her throat. Her mind raced. How should she answer him? All right, a sexual pull existed between them, but her talk of a romance had been frivolous and made in a kind of defiance. She had not meant it.

A split second later, she came to her senses. The shrug was just to tease and Jader did not mean anything either. His disapproval of her—of her mother—overruled any lust

he might feel and would cancel out thoughts of romance.
Period.

Ellen rose to her feet. 'I was talking in terms of the car
company,' she informed him, with as much dignity as she
could muster. 'And now I shall take a look in the kitchen
and see what I can make for dinner.'

CHAPTER THREE

A SECOND beautiful beach and another beautiful day. Raising her face to the sun, Ellen basked in its tropical warmth. She had always been a sun-worshipper and now she wanted to purr with pleasure. The top of the convertible was down, they were travelling along Ipanema and a light breeze was sifting playfully through her hair. They had just passed a digital signboard displaying temperature and time alternately, and it was twenty-six degrees and fourteen hundred hours.

Ellen had felt sure that after her prolonged daytime sleep yesterday, followed by a regular night's rest, she would be up and active early, but it had been one o'clock before her eyes had finally opened. She had showered, dressed and been drinking a cup of coffee out on the terrace when Jader had appeared.

'Spoilsport,' he had said, eyeing her slim figure in a sleeveless blue and white button-through dress.

'You returned unexpectedly in the hope of catching me without a stitch on? Better luck next time.' Ellen had flashed a smile. 'Though aren't you supposed to be tied up today?'

'I was, but I rushed through everything and managed to get away,' he had replied.

'So you could've taken me on a tour of the factory,' she had said pertly.

'So I will take you along the route you need to take to

reach Ipanema, stopping to buy an adaptor on the way,'
Jader had responded, and had gone on to suggest that they
travel down to the end of the beach and then double back
to Copacabana where they could have a late lunch.

'Sounds like fun,' Ellen had agreed, thinking that, even
if the factory seemed *verboten* to her, by taking the afternoon off and being the perfect host he was going all out
to please. She had given a dry smile. What a pity he had
an ulterior motive!

But being driven along in the sunshine *was* fun. Ellen
pushed her dark glasses higher up her nose. Backed by
verdant granite mountains, the long silver strand of beach
was seeded with clusters of gently waving palm trees. Lush
and graceful apartment blocks which looked as though
they should be featured in *Vogue* magazine lined the seafront, plus the occasional super deluxe hotel.

There were few bars and no shops; these were located
a block or two further back. Ipanema was more residential
and sophisticated than Copacabana, and not so busy, yet
it possessed a vibrancy. Fitness freaks who worked out on
the exercise bars called to each other, a youth selling corn
on the cob tooted a whistle to advertise his wares, sing-
song car horns peeped. And threaded through the cacoph-
ony of sound was music. Always music. In the past five
minutes, Ellen had heard the samba, bossa nova, a hum-
min' and a-strummin' hillbilly tune and even a snatch of
opera.

'Ipanema is Indian for dangerous waters,' Jader told her,
acting the role of tour guide.

He had glanced at the azure, white-crested waves which
were crashing onto the shore and Ellen followed his gaze.
Lithe-bodied surfers were riding the waves and further out
on the ocean sailboards with rainbow-coloured sails
bucked and rose, like so many aquatic butterflies.

'Is the water dangerous?' she enquired.

'There can be a strong undertow, so it's safer to stay in the shallows. Ipanema is considered to be a top place to live,' he went on, 'and the beach attracts intellectuals, teachers, writers who use it as a debating forum, a lecture hall, an office.'

'They hold cocktail parties too,' Ellen observed, for down on the sand a coterie of scantily garbed, smooth, bronzed types were milling around, brandishing drinks, smoking and avidly chattering. She brushed aside wisps of blonde hair which the breeze had tangled over her eyes. Rio's allure was legendary, and the people, the eternal summer scene and the music combined to create a sense of joy which was contagious. Ellen grinned. 'I like it here,' she declared.

'And they like you,' Jader said.

A truck performing an erratic five-point turn had brought the traffic to a queuing halt and on the pavement a few yards ahead a gang of wet-suited young Adonises were gazing approvingly in their direction.

'No,' Ellen said. 'They like the convertible.'

'It's you who's the *objet d'ogle*,' he insisted. 'See the guy who's nipping his earlobe between his thumb and finger? That means he thinks you're tasty—which you are.'

She smiled. Today was not a day for fighting shy of compliments; today was a day for accepting and enjoying them. 'Thank you, kind sir,' she said. 'But they noticed the car first.'

'Maybe,' Jader conceded. 'People frequently admire it.' Sliding a hand into the neck of his caramel-coloured sports shirt, he rubbed fractiously at the whorls of dark hair revealed in the V. 'However, unfortunately admiring is a very long way from buying.'

'The convertible has airbags, an electrically operated

vanishing hood, silent air-conditioning, and what other pulling points?' Ellen enquired.

'Wrap-around headlights, anti-lock braking system, side-impact bars to give protection if there should be an accident, and much more under the bonnet—which means getting technical. For example, limited slip differential.' He slung her a dry look. 'You wouldn't know what limited slip diff was if it jumped out and bit you on the ankle.'

'Not a chance,' she agreed. 'I have a car at home—a beat-up Ford—but all I do is sit behind the wheel and drive it.'

'Why do you want to know about the convertible?' Jader asked.

'Because I could write an article extolling its charms, perhaps from the viewpoint of the female driver, and try to get it published in Brazil.'

'Then people'll read your words and rush out to place orders in their thousands?' There was the springing arch of a nostril. 'Now why didn't I think of that?'

Ellen frowned. Writing an article had been an impromptu, off-the-top-of-her-head notion which was meant, first, to rattle Jader and, second—though perhaps mainly— to divert her attention from his fingers. Watching their rotation on his chest, she had found herself rapt and wondering how it would feel if his fingers were stroking over *her*. Yet perhaps an article would generate some interest?

'It could be useful,' she said, filled with sudden enthusiasm for the idea. 'And, after all, journalism is my forte and—' drawing her dark glasses down her nose, Ellen looked at him over the top '—we are pooling our resources.'

Jader bared his teeth in a smile which looked perilously close to a snarl. 'So you'd like to know everything there is to know about the convertible?'

'Please.'

'There's a brochure back at the apartment which you can read and I'll ask my secretary to amass the technical data, though I doubt she'll be able to manage it until after the holiday.'

'That's OK,' Ellen said, and looked at him sideways. Jader might appear to be courteously complying with her wishes, yet she was aware of him treading a narrow line between keeping her sweet and ordering her to get the hell out of his hair. She felt a pang. And maybe out of his life. 'I'm trying to help,' she protested.

'And not hinder?' He gave a swerved smile of scepticism. 'I wonder why I find that so hard to believe?'

In the distance, the truck roared off and the traffic started to move again. They continued along the seafront, passing over the canal which separated Ipanema from what Jader told her was Leblon, though it seemed to be a continuation of the same beach.

'Could you stop here, please?' Ellen requested, when an unusually long gap appeared amidst the line of cars which were parked at the kerb. 'I'd like to take some shots.'

He swung into the space and halted. 'You want a view of the shore?' he said.

'No, I want pictures of the convertible to illustrate my article,' she replied, bending to lift the camera bag which had been tucked in beside her feet. 'I need it standing on its own, in good light, and—'

Jader gunned the engine. 'We ought to be at the restaurant before three, so there isn't time right now,' he said, and, pulling down hard on the wheel, he hurled them back onto the road, performed a perfect U-turn and roared off again the way they had come.

'It would've only taken five minutes,' Ellen protested.

Her chauffeur turned to shine a regretful smile. 'I'm sorry.'

Fretting and fuming, she set her camera bag back down onto the floor. Jader was being deliberately uncooperative and, as with the factory tour, would doubtless go all out to thwart her in the future. But she needed a photograph of the convertible and, Ellen vowed mutinously, she would get one.

Situated in a large octagonal conservatory and with navy-clothed tables standing on a white tiled floor and bearing pristine white china, the restaurant was chic. Navy and white ceiling blinds kept out the glare of the sun, while pots of purple pelargoniums and scarlet hibiscus provided contrasting splashes of colour. The folding doors of one wall had been concertinaed aside, letting in the fresh air and giving a clear view of the pavement with its passers-by, the road and beyond it the turquoise-blue sea. Obviously a favourite eating place with locals, the restaurant also included a number of holidaymakers.

'Why not try a *caipirinha*? It's a lethal mixture of cane spirit, lime, crushed ice and sugar,' Jader said, when a young waiter in a navy pea jacket and white trousers came to take their orders for drinks. Ellen nodded her agreement. 'And *chopp*, draught beer, for me,' he said.

In double-quick time, their drinks were delivered and the waiter stood to attention. 'Today we serve our seafood buffet,' he announced, smiling at Ellen and speaking English on her behalf. He flourished an arm towards the back of the room. 'If you would care to help yourselves.'

'We will,' Jader told him.

Ellen took a sip of her drink. 'Delicious,' she said.

'Mine too,' Jader said, wiping froth from his mouth with the back of his hand.

The buffet table was a work of art. Huge clawed lobsters, pyramids of pink shrimp and brown-shelled crabs formed a centre-piece, while on either side were platters of cooked red snapper, a multitude of other fishes, oysters and smoked salmon. Bowls of salad, tomatoes, sliced avocado, coleslaws and sauces filled the outer fringes. On a separate table stood the desserts—chocolate gateau, mango mousse, crème brûlée, cream meringues... The choice went on and on.

The food was tasty and Ellen had to admit that no matter how infuriating he might be, and even if he was only tolerating her presence, Jader made a good companion. As they ate, he asked her about newspaper assignments she had been on and showed such interest that she soon found herself chattering. The conversation moved on effortlessly to places they had visited, books they had read and films they had seen.

They were drinking cups of *cafezinho*, which was thick dark coffee, when Ellen tilted her head. For a while she had heard the gentle throb of drums in the background, but the sound was coming closer. Looking out at the road, she saw a band of drummers and percussion players march into view, followed by a troupe of men and girls.

Totalling around a hundred people, band and troupe were dressed alike. The men wore gold satin shirts, silver Lurex trousers, tailcoats and top hats, while the girls were clad in gold satin boob tubes, skimpy silver shorts and top hats. All dancing in time, they were as professional as a Broadway chorus line.

'It's a samba school,' Jader told her, when she eyed them with delight. 'They're practising for the Carnival parade.'

Designating the diners as their audience, the procession halted, swivelled to face the restaurant and, after a dramatic roll on the drums, launched into a new routine. Legs kicked, top hats were juggled, girls did the splits. The performance oozed across the dual carriageway, bringing traffic to a total standstill. If anyone was in a hurry, they could forget it! A plump, moustached policeman appeared, but instead of ordering the samba school to move to one side, as Ellen expected, he flattened a hand on his midriff and started to swing his hips.

The rhythm was infectious and the music seemed to penetrate the bones. Outside, the crowd which had gathered was swaying. Kids bongo-drummed in tandem on the bonnets of stationary cars. Of its own accord, Ellen's foot had begun to move and Jader's fingers were thrumming on the table. Someone in the restaurant tapped a spoon against their cup and, in seconds, everyone was tapping to the rhythm—spoons on cups, forks on plates, knives on glasses.

They grinned at each other.

'A magic moment,' Ellen said.

Jader reached out to take hold of her hand. 'It could only happen in Rio.'

She nodded, and waited. She expected him to release her hand, but instead he linked his fingers closer with hers. For a moment, Ellen wondered if she should pull free, but decided against it. A great good humour floated all around and to be sitting holding hands as they watched the samba school together seemed…appro-priate.

Something inside her tingled. Perhaps the hot-blooded, anything-goes spirit of the city was seeping in, but a holiday romance seemed appropriate too. Her love affairs had been widely spaced in time and only entered into after much serious deliberation on her part, but—for once—why didn't she throw caution to the winds? She was a long way from home, in Brazil on a one-off visit, and adult and single. A romantic interlude would do no harm, yet it could add a sparkle to her love life, which, Ellen had to admit, was lacklustre.

She poked at a pellet of silver foil, crumpled up from her after-meal mint. Before a romance could begin, she required a partner. Someone in his thirties with, perhaps, thick dark brown hair which fell over his brow. Who had a faint shadow on his jaw and would need to shave once if not twice a day. A man with powerful shoulders, lean hips, who was well toned physically. And mentally, too, for he must be smart, witty and nobody's fool. Someone who—

'Bravo!' a woman shouted from behind.

Ellen jolted back to life. The samba school was starting on an even more frenetic number, but she had not been watching them; she had been gazing at Jader. She had been cataloguing *his* attributes. The *caipirinha* was not only lethal, it softened the brain!

'My camera,' Ellen said, snatching her hand from his and hastily opening the bag. 'This is the ideal chance for photographs.'

She rushed outside where, amidst a phalanx of amateur photographers, she became busy taking shots. Ellen snapped multi-peopled pictures, lone dancers, a close-up of a top hat being tipped from a curly brown head. And when the members of the samba school took their bows she sped rapidly backwards in order to capture the entire group.

'You seemed to get what you wanted,' Jader remarked, when the procession had moved off and she returned to their table.

Ellen nodded happily. 'A good selection, and the shiny costumes'll add pizzazz. You talked about us going to a fancy-dress ball. Are we supposed to wear costumes?' she asked.

'There's a choice. It's either black tie and evening dress or you can deck yourself out to fit the theme of the ball, which is the Roaring Twenties. Or that's the theory,' Jader told her, 'but I gather that in practice the whole thing's free and easy, and people dress however the mood takes them.'

'You haven't been to a carnival ball before?'

He shook his head. 'Never. But a couple of guys I knew at school, Marco and Nilson, now live in Rio and we're making up a party with them and their wives. The ball starts around eleven and goes through until five a.m. or later—'

'Phew!'

Jader grinned. 'It'll take stamina—and apparently it's one of the most lavish. According to Anna—she's Marco's wife—Brazilian TV celebrities often attend, together with big names from the rock music fraternity, plus some from Hollywood. She reckons Roscoe Chard might be going.'

'Big deal,' Ellen remarked drily. Square-jawed, blond and with a toothpaste-white smile, the American movie star was a blockbusting romantic lead and an international idol. He had recently won an Oscar for his performance as a suave, oily-smooth lawyer, though in her opinion he had been playing himself—as he invariably did. 'I seem to remember reading that Roscoe Chard owned a holiday home in Rio,' she said.

'He does,' Jader confirmed, and grimaced. 'The guy loves to be noticed, so whenever he's in town there are pictures of him in the papers—driving around in his custom-sprayed purple coupé or arriving at nightclubs with some pouting bimbo hung on his arm.'

'Will your friends be in fancy dress?' Ellen asked, wondering what she was going to wear.

She did not own an evening dress but the ones she had

seen in the windows of Rio's boutiques had been extrav-
agant, expensive-looking confections, and she knew that if
she bought one she would never wear it again. She had
brought clothes for the evening—a cream embroidered
full-sleeved shirt, jewel-coloured waistcoat, filmy blue-
grey blouse and matching palazzo pants—but they were
relatively subdued and, she suspected, would look ordinary
at the ball. Ellen squeezed the foil pellet between her fingers. Looking ordinary did not appeal.

'I believe so, of some kind,' Jader said. 'But don't
worry; Anna's given me the name of a store which hires
out outfits. It's just around the corner and we'll go along
there as soon as you're ready.'

Lifting her cup, Ellen drank the last inch of coffee. She
was eager to organise an outfit. 'I'm ready now,' she declared.

A select establishment of wood-panelled walls, fir-green
carpet and with the aura of a baronial hall, the shop sold
regular fashions on the ground floor, while fancy-dress outfits were kept on the first. Downstairs assistants were at-
tending to a number of customers, but when they mounted
the staircase the floor which stretched ahead of them was
deserted.

'*Boa tarde,*' smiled a middle-aged mulatto woman in
the regulation smart black dress, who had emerged from a
side-room to greet them.

'*Boa tarde,*' Jader replied.

He explained their mission in Portuguese, but as she
listened the woman's face fell and, with gestures towards
the half-empty rails which surrounded the room, she gar-
rulously answered him.

'She's saying we've left it late and now there's very
little choice,' he translated.

Ellen took a step towards a velour-clad rail. 'But I need something,' she said.

Rushing ahead, the assistant showed her a stiff, spangled, plum-coloured crinoline. 'You like this?' she asked, in heavily accented English.

Ellen smiled and shook her head. She did not like it, nor would she ever squeeze the huge skirt through a door, let alone into the car. *'Não, obrigada,'* she replied.

The woman riffled through items on the rail. 'This?' she said hopefully.

Jader chuckled. 'Now that,' he said, 'is perfect.'

'Ha, ha,' Ellen said, and wrinkled her nose at him. 'Whilst I haven't majored in the subject, to the best of my knowledge the Pink Panther didn't exist in the Roaring Twenties.'

'Ah, you want for Twenties?' the assistant said, as though this solved everything. 'I bring dress for you in the—' She pointed to a trio of curtained-off cubicles at the far end of the floor.

'Changing room,' Jader said.

Next the assistant pointed to a sofa. 'You, *senhor*, sit there.'

Ellen had shed her dress and was standing in her bra and bikini briefs when the assistant appeared through the curtains. She held a couple of items in her hand, while what looked like a bundle of black lace was draped over one arm.

'Off, *obrigada*,' she instructed, pointing at Ellen's bra, and because compliance was expected she obeyed. The lacy garment was held out. 'On, *obrigada*.' Again, Ellen obeyed. She stepped in, a zip was drawn up, the assistant added accessories. A minute or two later, the woman clapped her hands together. 'Fantastic!' she declared.

Ellen eyed herself dubiously in the full-length mirror.

She was wearing a diamanté headband, with feather, black fishnet hold-up stockings with lacy tops, and a white satin basque covered in heavy black lace. She had never worn a basque before, never worn hold-up stockings before.

All of a sudden, Ellen grinned. She had never felt so glamorous or so sexy. She lifted her head, straightened her shoulders and smiled. The siren who was her reflection smiled confidently back. This was a woman who could bust male heartstrings by the hundred and revel in it. This was a woman who knew she looked good and regarded compliments as her right.

Glancing down at Ellen's stockinged feet, the assistant stepped out of her black high-heeled shoes and indicated that she should wear them. Ellen did as instructed. She smiled at her reflection again. The shoes were a couple of sizes too big, but the lift of the heels imparted an even headier panache.

'Come,' the shop assistant said. 'You show your man.'

Ellen drew in a breath, pushed aside the curtain and strode out into the shop. Jader was leafing idly through a magazine, but he looked up to gaze at her in silence.

'Fantastic?' the assistant demanded, giving Ellen a conspiratorial smile.

Jader placed a hand on his brow. 'Pass the smelling salts—I think I'm going to faint,' he said.

The woman laughed. She did not understand what he had said, but the gesture made his meaning abundantly clear. She was beaming and proudly taking credit for Ellen's transformation, when a telephone shrilled in the side-room.

'Excuse me,' she said, and rushed off.

'From sweet gentility to sudden raunch,' Jader murmured.

'You like it?' Ellen asked.

'It beats the hell out of the Pink Panther,' he said.

She grinned and, boosted by the admiration which she saw in his eyes, started to perform a pirouette. 'I've never— Oh!' she gasped.

Unsteady in the too large shoes, as Ellen had swivelled she'd snagged a needle-thin heel in the carpet. Her foot had slid sideways, the heel had tipped and she felt herself falling. She was clawing at thin air, when Jader leapt from the sofa, caught her in his arms and held her upright.

She clung onto his shoulders. 'Thank—thank you,' she said, flushed-faced and panting.

Jader smiled, then his eyes fell to travel across the smoothness of her shoulders and down to the impetuous rise and fall of her breasts. He stood perfectly still and slowly, slowly, and as if he could not help himself, raised a hand and trailed his fingertips gently from the base of her throat and down. As his touch moved over one honeyed curve, into the dip between her breasts and across the other, Ellen's senses sang. She had wondered how it would feel if Jader stroked her, and it felt like bliss.

'It's not the Twenties,' she said, her voice unconsciously husky.

He looked up. He seemed dazed. 'What? No, it's more the Wild West in the 1800s.' Placing his hands at her waist, Jader held her a little away from him. He grinned. 'You look like you've just sashayed out of a bordello.'

Ellen stiffened. Why did he have to say that?

'A bor—bordello?' she repeated uncertainly.

'You look like a gorgeous, high-class tart,' he told her, and growled deep in his throat. 'Most appealing.'

Ellen took a decisive step backwards, which forced him to release her. 'I want to dress for the era,' she said.

'But no one gives a damn about the era,' Jader demurred.

She turned and marched back into the cubicle, going as fast as she could in the high heels. 'I do,' she declared, and, with a hasty swish, she drew the curtain closed.

Ellen peeled off the basque and was fully dressed again when the assistant came in.

'I'd like to take these,' she told her, indicating the diamanté headband and the stockings. She did not really want them, but the woman had been so pleasant and helpful that she felt she ought to buy something.

The assistant picked up the discarded basque. 'You no want this?' she asked, in surprise. 'You change your mind?'

'*Sim.* I don't know what I'll wear for the ball,' Ellen said ruefully.

'You wear bra and panties, and—' there was a mental translation into English '—suspender belt.'

'That's all?' she protested.

The woman nodded. 'It seem not much? OK, but you are young and slim, so why not—what is the saying—live a little?'

Ellen's purchases were wrapped in black tissue paper and placed in a baby-pink box, and she paid the bill.

'I'd like to take a few more photographs,' she told Jader as they left the shop. 'Do you think we could walk along Copacabana for a while?'

'Sure,' he agreed, and they made their way back to the seafront and crossed onto the mosaic pavement. He offered to carry the box while Ellen dealt with her camera. 'You lost your nerve?' Jader enquired, when she stopped to fit a lens.

'Sorry?'

'You didn't have the courage to wear the basque, the bustier, whatever it was called?'

Ellen concentrated on the lens. 'I had the courage, but

the outfit had no connection with the Twenties. That's why I changed my mind,' she vowed.

Jader gave her a wry smile. 'I believe you,' he said, though it was clear he did not believe her at all.

'The assistant suggested I wear just a bra, panties and suspender belt for the ball,' Ellen told him as they started to walk again.

'Apparently women often do—' he grinned '—and some of the guys who dress up as women. But it can get very hot and sticky, so it makes sense to wear the minimum.' He cast her a glance. 'You're not inclined to take up the suggestion?'

Ellen visualised her cotton underwear which, whilst as white and fresh as newly fallen snow, had been chosen more for serviceability than for glamour. 'No,' she replied, and frowned. Could remnants of her plain Jane phase still remain?

Jader saw her frown. 'Perhaps you'd prefer to skip the ball? I understand things can sometimes get a little wild and—' his drawl teasingly mocked her '—they're not for the puritanical or faint-hearted.'

'I'm neither puritanical nor faint-hearted,' Ellen declared. 'I wouldn't miss it for the world. I *want* to go to the ball.'

He bowed a solemn head. 'Cinderella's wish shall be granted.'

Focusing her camera on the long-distance view, Ellen operated the shutter. 'Is Prince Charming going to wear women's underwear?' she asked.

Jader made a face. 'No, I'll stick to boring shirt and shorts.'

'How about tying a black bow-tie around your neck and wearing a G-string?' she suggested, recalling posters she had seen advertising a male dance group which performed erotic routines.

He shuddered. 'No, thanks.'

'Spoilsport,' Ellen said, and had a reckless mental image of him—not as a dancer—Jader was too grittily male and self-contained for that—but naked and lying on a bed. Something inside her contracted. With his dark Latin looks, golden skin and lean physique, he would be a magnificent male animal. Chances were he was also a good lover.

Stop it right there, Ellen ordered herself, and, sturdily rejecting her thoughts, she photographed a passing car which was smothered in balloons, then halted to line up a shot of a toothless old man with a bandana slipping over one ear who was selling kites on the beach.

'I don't know why I didn't recognise you at the airport,' Jader remarked as she waited for the man to come closer. 'You have a definite look of your mother.'

As always when the likeness was mentioned, Ellen felt a tension rise within her. 'So I've been told.' There was a tiny beat, and she said, 'Though my mouth's fuller—'

'You have a sulky, sexy bottom lip,' he murmured.

'And I have a bump on my nose.'

'I've not noticed it,' Jader protested.

'There,' she said, showing him.

'Infinitesimal.'

'And my mother is always neat and tidy, whereas—' Ellen shoved a hand through her tousled mane of blonde hair '—I'm much messier.'

'Maybe, but you're also…gutsier. A fighter. You have a firm grip on life,' he said thoughtfully, 'while Vivienne was a little remote. I felt she had a melancholy quality, a core of sadness. Perhaps because your father had been killed so tragically?'

'Perhaps,' Ellen said, being scrupulously noncom-mittal.

'You said Vivienne's known the man she's married for a long time; did she meet him when she was in Paris?'

Ellen felt a stab of disquiet. She supposed it had been inevitable that Jader would bring up her mother's past some time during her stay, but she had not imagined he would choose to do so in public. She stared blindly into the view-finder. It was not something she wished to discuss out on the street or right now. Before they delved into the subject—before Jader thrashed her with it—she needed to collect her thoughts, do a mental trial run of possible conversations and adopt a cool composure.

'That's right,' Ellen replied.

'How did you enjoy living in Paris?' Jader enquired.

'I didn't live there. I stayed with my grandparents, my father's parents, in Kent,' she said, making herself concentrate on the kite-seller.

'How long were you with them?'

'From the age of eighteen months until I was twelve.'

'All those years?' Jader raised surprised brows. 'Conrado said that when Vivienne was in Paris her work took her to Spain, Greece, the Middle East,' he continued.

Ellen's stomach churned. She felt ill. You can cope with this, she told herself as if reciting a mantra. You've coped before.

'From time to time,' she said as the figure in the view-finder became larger, clearer.

'Did Vivienne ever take you with her on her visits?'

She had been about to press the button, but now Ellen lowered her camera to give him a frowning look. 'It wouldn't have been suitable.'

'But it would've given the two of you a chance to be together on a sort of holiday and I can't see that the occasional visit would've hurt,' Jader protested. 'The Arabs, in particular, love kids and I'd have thought that Vivienne taking along a little blonde daughter might've coaxed them to buy paintings or sell them, whichever the deal was, even more willingly.'

Ellen stared at him. 'Um—perhaps. But—but I never went along,' she faltered, and, raising her camera, she took hurried shots of the retreating kite-seller.

The shots were out of focus, but she did not notice. Only one thought thrummed in her head: that Jader did not know the truth. Did not know! His ignorance came as a total shock, like being hit by a ten-ton truck which she had not seen approaching.

Ellen's brain whirled. She had always taken it for granted that Conrado had revealed all to his son, but he must have felt unable to bring himself to share a truth which he might have believed made him look a fool and shamed him. It was understandable, she acknowledged, and her mind stumbled. But if Jader did not know the truth, then his disapproval could not come through her mother to her; it must come directly *at* her.

Ellen's brow creased. Jader had been violently critical of her supposed motives in ending the relationship between his father and her mother ten years ago, yet time was said to heal and it astonished her that he should still be hostile. Should she tell him what she had told Conrado and clear her name, or maintain the silence and run the gauntlet of his hostility?

Opening the bag, Ellen stashed her camera away. If Conrado had concealed the truth for all these years, then keeping quiet had mattered to him. Mattered profoundly. So, out of respect for the wishes and the memory of the man for whom she had cared so much, she would keep quiet too.

CHAPTER FOUR

ELLEN'S footsteps took an abrupt curving swerve. She walked across the forecourt of the car showroom and, raising a hand to shade her eyes, peered in through the plate-glass window. A chuckle bubbled gleefully up from her throat. After a day filled with one satisfying episode after another, she had chanced upon what could prove to be the most satisfying episode of them all!

On his way to work that morning, Jader had dropped her off in the heart of the city. There she had snapped stalls laden with papaya, pineapple and other exotic fruits, a boy on a skateboard hanging onto a car bumper and hitching a free ride, two stilt-walkers nonchalantly playing trombones amongst the kamikaze traffic. Commandeering a cab, she had proceeded on to Santa Teresa, a quiet neighbourhood of cobbled streets and decaying colonial mansions which had echoes of Lisbon. It was a haven for artists—and heaven for the tourist-cum-photographer.

A visit to the Botanical Gardens had come next. Founded in 1808 and the oldest in the western hemisphere, the gardens had provided a tranquil stroll through avenues of stately palms and shots of flamboyant tropical plants.

Starting to weary and being in the vicinity, Ellen had returned to the apartment. Although Jader had told her he would be spending a full day at the office, she had wondered whether he might come back in the early afternoon again, but he was nowhere around. After eating a late

snack lunch, she had left a note saying she had gone to
Ipanema. At the beach, half a reel of film had been used
before she'd stretched her towel out on the sand, shed the
dress which covered her bikini and lain down. A dozy
sunbathing session had followed.

But now, taking a parallel street to the one which they
had driven down the previous day, Ellen was on her way
back to the apartment. And now she was looking at another
Moreira convertible, a metallic green one with a cream soft
top this time.

She pushed her way in through double swing doors.
With a white maple floor, black pillars decorated with
sleek steel shapes and a cantilevered glass roof, the showroom was large and modernistic. There was sufficient light
for her to photograph the convertible, though as it stood—
in the back row of three rows of cars and between two
low-slung sports models—it would be difficult to frame on
its own. Ellen walked forward. But if one of the sports
models could be moved a few yards—

'*Boa tarde.*'

A doughy, bespectacled young man in a navy suit and
yellow polka-dotted bow-tie had risen from behind a stainless-steel desk which sat discreetly against one wall. He
immediately bowled into an obvious salesman's welcoming spiel, but his speech was lisping and rapid, and she
could not follow. Indeed, he might as well have been
speaking in Urdu.

As he reached her, Ellen smiled and, in her best
Portuguese, asked if he spoke English.

The young man nodded. 'You betcha,' he said.

'I'd like to take a photograph of this car,' she told him,
weaving her way through to the rear of the showroom
where she indicated the Moreira.

'Photograph before test drive?' he enquired.

'No, I'd just like to take a photograph.' Ellen smiled her sweetest smile—a smile which had allowed her to snap the most reluctant of subjects and convince the strenuously unwilling that they should grant her an interview. 'Would that be OK?'

The salesman grinned and smoothed down his hair. 'Just photograph?' he said, puzzled.

'Yes. I've already driven in the car,' she added, 'and I don't want to buy one.'

He looked confused. 'Not buy?'

'No. I come from England—' Ellen hesitated, aware of having already said too much unnecessarily and wondering how she could explain what was a complicated situation '—and actually I'm a shareholder and—'

'A shareholder?'

She nodded. 'I own shares in the car company.'

'Ah,' the young man said, tapping the side of his nose with a pudgy finger. 'I dig.' He stepped back and spread his arms out wide. 'Please, take photograph. Take many photographs.'

'Thank you, but there's a problem, Would it be possible for you to steer that car—' she pointed '—aside, and move this one—' she touched the convertible's bonnet '—into the space?' Ellen smiled another sweet smile. *'Por favor?'*

'You betcha,' the salesman said again, making her wonder if he might have learned his English from American movies. 'I get the keys.' Returning to his desk, he searched rapidly through the drawers. 'One moment,' he said, with a whirl of hands which signified that the keys must be elsewhere, and disappeared out through a door at the back.

Left alone, Ellen put her camera bag and plastic carrier down on the desk, and wandered slowly off amongst the cars. The salesman had seemed most impressed when she'd told him she was a shareholder, she reflected. As if it made her a very important person. Her train of thought jumped tracks. Jader must have been astonished when he'd discovered that Conrado had left her the shares. Her mouth curved into a wry smile. And furious. And apoplectic.

She strolled towards the front of the showroom. Yet had he never wondered why his father should make such a magnanimous gesture? Didn't he—?

At the sudden squeal of tyres, Ellen looked up. Outside on the sunny street, a car had come to a halt and its driver was climbing out. Her stomach muscles clenched. The car was the scarlet convertible and the man heading for the showroom—and for her—was Jader. Damn it. As she gazed at him, it registered that he must have been back to the apartment after work, for he wore a short-sleeved khaki shirt and khaki trousers. It also registered that her heart was beating traitorously fast.

'I've been looking for you everywhere,' Jader said as he came in through the swing doors. 'What's the matter? Did you get lost and are you asking...?' His words died. He had looked beyond her and spotted the green convertible. 'What stunt are you pulling?' he demanded.

Ellen's chin lifted. He might have caught her in the act, but she refused to be daunted. And if anger was darkening his brown eyes and adding a granite edge to his jaw, so what?

'There's no stunt,' she replied, keeping her voice determinedly matter-of-fact. 'I'm simply arranging to take a photograph of the Moreira. I'm sorry if that doesn't make you jump for joy and blow whistles, but I said I was determined—'

'You are,' he rasped. 'You're determined to interfere and to hell with whatever harm you might cause to anyone else!'

Ellen frowned. Although Jader appeared to be speaking

about now, she sensed that he could also be recalling what he regarded as her interference of ten years ago and was castigating her for that too. Her spine stiffened. But he had mistaken her motivation then and, in being against an article, he was mistaken now.

'You want to smack me?' she enquired, holding out a hand.

Jader smiled, cold as ice. 'Don't tempt me,' he said, 'though it's your backside which—'

He stopped at the sound of conversation behind them. The salesman had come back into the showroom, accompanied by an older, thinner man in overalls who looked like a mechanic. As they walked towards the convertible, the salesman was jabbering away to his companion and gesturing towards Ellen. When he saw that she was looking at him, he shone her a broad smile. Ellen smiled back. As before, his lisping, quickfire Portuguese was impenetrable, though oddly the words 'Rolls-Royce', 'Jaguar' and 'Bentley' did emerge.

'You told him you owned shares in a British car company?' Jader demanded.

Ellen looked at him in surprise. 'No.'

'He thinks you did.' Folding muscled arms across his chest and standing with his long legs apart, he adopted a critical stance. 'He seems to believe you're a sizeable shareholder in one of the UK firms which manufacture quality cars.'

'I never said that,' she protested. 'He's misunderstood.'

Jader listened to more of the ongoing conversation. 'And the general impression is that you're involved in some kind of fact-finding mission to discover which direction the car industry is going in Brazil.'

Ellen imagined how she must look—young, casually

dressed and tousled after sunbathing on the beach. She laughed. 'That's absurd,' she said.

'Not as absurd as you coming in here to photograph a Moreira,' Jader retorted.

'I had no alternative.'

His lips shut tight, like the edges of an iron box. 'You did.'

'You mean that if I'd asked nicely you'd have let me photograph your car?' Ellen shook her head. 'I don't think so.'

'I mean you could have abandoned your idea of writing an article,' Jader grated. 'However, it's bloody obvious that's not going to happen and that if I stop you here you'll track down another Moreira in another showroom. Then you'll use your womanly wiles to coax some other poor sucker to do your bidding,' he continued, and made an angry swipe with his hands, 'so I give up.'

Ellen gave him a doubtful look. 'Give up?' she repeated uncertainly. He was not the type to back down on anything, so could this be a trick? 'You're allowing me to snap your car?'

'From every angle, *querida*,' Jader replied, though the word was not an endearment.

She looked across at where the salesman had climbed into the driving seat of one of the sports cars, while the mechanic was preparing to push.

'Please would you tell them not to bother?' she said.

'I'm even expected to do your dirty work for you?' Jader protested, but he called across something to the men which made them cease their efforts, shake their heads at her and shrug.

'You told them I'm a neurotic, bubble-brained blonde who is given to rash impulses?' Ellen asked, when she had collected her bags and they had gone outside.

'Something similar,' Jader said tersely.

She frowned at him and turned to frown at the convertible. 'Is there a car wash anywhere near?' she enquired. 'The bodywork's picked up a film of dust and it'll photograph far better if it's clean and glossy.'

'There's one a few blocks away,' Jader replied, wrenching open his door with far more force than was necessary. 'I suppose you want to go there right now?'

Ellen shone him a smile. She could not be certain that his sudden concession would last and it seemed wise to act quickly, before he changed his mind. 'If it's not too much trouble.'

'For you, anything,' he said pithily.

When they arrived, the car wash was empty. Jader bought a token at the kiosk and, as they drove round to the bay, raised and secured the soft-top roof.

'Windows,' he said, inserting the plastic token into the acceptor and driving forward to stop at the floor bar. 'You'll be pleased to hear that I chose gold service, which means we're having foam wash, wheel brush, underchassis wash, hot wax, the works,' he informed her, his tone sardonic.

'Thanks.' Ellen had taken the car brochure which he had given her down to the beach, and now she had retrieved it from her bag and was looking at it. 'I've started to translate this,' she said as he switched off the engine, 'but I need to keep referring to the dictionary and it takes ages, so I was wondering—' She gave him an appealing glance.

In a gesture of frustration, Jader grasped the steering wheel with two large hands and dropped down his head so that his forehead was resting on the upper curve. 'If this poor sucker would translate it for you?' he demanded, through clenched teeth.

'Well…parts.' Ellen tried him with a smile, but he ignored her. As the wash machinery started towards them and water rattled on the bonnet, she gazed at the brochure. If Jader refused to help, translation was destined to be a tiresome and lengthy process. And once the article had been written in English her words would need to be changed straight back into Portuguese. 'It says something here about the convertible making a statement— Cripes!'

A torrent of cold, soapy rain was pouring in on her. Ellen raised the brochure in a frantic attempt to shield herself, but the water bounced off and past, hosing down her hair, her face, her dress. She was flinching against the squirting spray when it was replaced by a massive shaggy red roller. 'Yuck!' she shrieked. The water had been bad enough, but the roller was worse. It lurched into the car to lick over her with a thousand sudsy spaniel tongues. Ellen cowered back in her seat, but the tongues followed, enthusiastically slavering.

'Close your window,' Jader said, and she realised he was laughing.

Ellen blinked desperately through the flicking, licking, soapy saliva. 'What? How?' she squawked.

'Press—the button—' chuckles of deep male laughter were interspersing his words '—on—your door.'

'Where?' She made a blind, slithery fumble. 'Oh, yes.' She pressed and, as the roller trawled off to rotate over the back of the car, the window sailed serenely up.

Ellen smeared a hand across her wet cheeks, gathering drips. The passage of the spray and the roller must have taken less than a minute, but a mass of chemical froth clung to her hair, her dress resembled an oozing rag, water streamed from her arms and legs. Hearing herself squelch in her seat, she turned to look at Jader. Damp spots on his shirt and flecks of foam which showed white against the darkness of his hair gave evidence that he had been splashed too; but only a little.

'Hard luck,' he said, and although it demanded a visible effort he stopped laughing, yet a grin persisted.

'Hard luck nothing! You knew I hadn't closed my window,' Ellen accused furiously. 'You realised I was going to be soaked, but instead of warning me you let it happen. You—you slimeball! And I *am* soaked, from head to foot,' she declared, plucking angrily at the sodden skirt of her dress. 'I'm also sitting in a pool of water. My shoes are wet and my hair'll need to be washed—if it doesn't drop out, because I dread to think what damage the detergent will've done to it.

'I suppose you decided you'd teach me a lesson?' she stormed on. 'Well, you might regard it as very funny, but I think it stinks!'

'Are you finished?' Jader asked.

'No, I'm not,' Ellen snapped, and brandished a fist.

She was meaning to punch him in the ribs, hard, but he realised her intention and, with what seemed insulting ease, caught hold of her wrist and stopped her.

'I didn't smack you and you won't hit me,' he said, in a low, firm voice. 'Even if you are the hellcat of all time.'

Ellen drew in a ragged breath. 'I'm sorry. You can let me go. I don't believe in violence,' she said as he released her, 'and I've never attempted to inflict any grievous bodily harm on anyone before. I'm not usually so—'

'Passionate?' Jader suggested, when she stopped to find a suitable word.

'Maybe,' Ellen muttered.

Although she held positive views and was not afraid of standing up for herself, she had not believed it was in her nature to get so carried away. Yet, for a moment, the pure white flame of anger had consumed her. Ellen glanced down. 'Passionate' also had a sexual connotation, which made her aware of how her sodden dress was clinging like a second skin and how, after the surprisingly cold douche of the water, her nipples were erect.

She shot a look at Jader and saw from the dip of his gaze that he was noticing her 'passionate' appearance too. She gritted her teeth. Would he comment?

'Whilst it *was* funny,' Jader said, brushing the foam flecks from his hair, 'I did tell you to close your window and I hadn't noticed it was still open.'

'OK,' Ellen said, recognising that her accusation had been rash and untrue.

'I wasn't teaching you a lesson,' he continued, and looked at the brochure which lay soggily in her lap, 'though if your ardour for writing about the car has been dampened—good.'

Ellen did not reply.

As the roller pummelled back over the roof and twirled moistly down the windscreen on its return journey, she reached into the bag for her towel. Water had seeped in to wet the edges, but it was mostly dry. She wiped her face and scrubbed the foam from her hair.

'What are you doing?' Jader enquired, when she started to undo the buttons at the front of her blue and white dress.

'I'm taking it off,' Ellen said.

His forehead furrowed. 'But—'

'I'm wearing my bikini, so I'll travel back in that.' The wet cotton felt uncomfortable against her skin and her bikini would not reveal much more, she had rationalised. Peeling off the dress, she put it into the bag. 'It's a bikini I brought with me,' Ellen went on as she lifted her hips and mopped up the puddle on her seat, 'so I'm wearing a lot more than most of the girls I saw on the beach.'

'I guess,' Jader muttered.

Sitting down again, she began to rub her hair. 'Earlier you talked about me causing harm to others. How could an article cause any harm?' Ellen asked curiously.

The rollers had completed their performance and flutes were approaching, shooting out hot air and blowing diamond drops of water across the windscreen.

'Because whatever you write is going to be interpreted as an advertising feature,' he said. 'And, as employing agencies is expensive and they weren't boosting sales, we've stopped advertising and so, no matter what I say, the workforce may view your article as an alternative effort and a symbol of hope. I'm not saying they would, only that they could because everyone's starting to clutch at straws. And I'm reluctant to have hopes raised—and dashed.'

Ellen considered this. 'I don't want to upset your workers and so I won't write an article,' she told him.

'The voice of reason, at last,' Jader said heavily. 'Thank you.'

'Why didn't you explain about me raising false hopes before?' she demanded.

'Because, frankly, I didn't think it'd make one iota of difference.'

'Of course it would,' she protested. 'I'm a sensitive human being. I don't ride roughshod over other people's feelings. I'd never bowl ahead and do what I wanted if it meant someone else might suffer in consequence.'

'Is that so?' Jader said, and she recognised a reference to the past.

'It is,' Ellen replied firmly. She put the towel away in her bag. 'If I could write about a news event which happened to involve the car, that wouldn't be an advertisement and it wouldn't raise false hopes,' she mused. 'Yet it might create an interest in the Moreira.'

'What do you have in mind?' He thrust her a dry look. 'Man driven to end of tether by contrary blonde drives off high cliff?'

'Doesn't have enough impact,' Ellen informed him crisply. 'Aren't we free to go now?' she asked, a minute or so later.

The hot-air flutes had retreated, the machinery stood still and silent, and a green light had come on. But Jader was continuing to look at her and had not noticed.

'*Sim,*' he agreed, in surprise, and pushed into gear.

As they shot somewhat erratically out of the car wash, Ellen smothered a grin. Her topaz-coloured bikini might be more substantial than the itsy-bitsy strands of 'dental floss' sported by many of the local girls, yet it revealed sufficient of her curves for him to be fascinated.

Impishly, she sat straighter and was aware of Jader shooting a sideways glance at the curve of her breasts, followed by him frowning and restlessly changing his position. Ellen's grin broke free. He might have been amused by her nudity in the kitchen, but, seated in the close confines of the car, it was obvious that he found her semi-nude presence disturbing.

'Wouldn't you be warmer with the towel wrapped around you?' Jader suggested as they drove along.

'I'm fine,' she declared casually.

Sliding one hand to the back of her neck, Ellen lifted the weight of blonde hair from her nape. A stray breeze had wafted and was cooling her skin. She sighed. Delicious. They might be sitting in the open air beside a large swimming pool and beneath a moonlit sky, but the crowds which filled the close-packed tables and shimmied on the dance-floor generated a powerful heat.

Ellen's lips tweaked. As the air temperature had been

raised, so a combination of throbbing beat, Carnival exuberance and an astonishing amount of bare flesh meant that the night's erotic temperature had soared too.

She was not immune to it and—she cast a glance at Jader, who was sitting beside her and currently talking to Anna—neither was he. They might both be wary of the physical attraction which jangled between them, yet this evening they were less wary, Ellen mused. This evening, they seemed to have reached a silent mutual acceptance that it existed. This evening they had danced close together, laughingly hugged each other and, even as he spoke to Anna, Jader was holding her hand.

Ellen slid a covert look at her escort. He wore a white cotton shirt with the sleeves rolled up above his elbows and close-fitting denim shorts—shorts which flattered his neat rear end and revealed strong golden thighs with a sprinkling of dark hair. The heat had added a sheen of moisture to his skin and stuck his shirt fast to his back. Her pulse rate quickened. The sweat and tumble of damp dark hair over his brow gave Jader an earthy quality which appealed to her.

Slicing off such disturbing thoughts, Ellen turned and, as it had done throughout the evening, her gaze circled around the fairy-lit dance-floor and the streamer-strewn tables. A heady mix of glamour and gaiety, the ball gave new meaning to the term 'nightlife'.

Yes, there were women clad in bras and suspender belts, and in other flimsy lingerie confections, including basques. And similarly attired cross-dressed men. Amongst the throng, she saw girls wearing bodypaint and a scatter of strategically placed sequins, drag queens in masks and chains, would-be Tarzans sporting leopardskin jockstraps and not much else.

At first, she had looked askance at the more X-rated

outfits, but in time she had become used to them. Whether they were slender or voluptuous, the women, in particular, were proud to present themselves—and why not?

Ellen's survey continued. She could see no sign of Roscoe Chard, but, so the movie-star-struck Anna had informed her, the celebrities often did a circuit of the more fashionable balls, and maybe he had yet to arrive. However, she had identified two other actors, a playboy millionaire and a shaven-headed girl whom she remembered from a heavy metal rock group.

Noticing a velvet ballgown and a couple of men in dinner jackets, Ellen grimaced. It would be amazing if their wearers survived the night without collapsing from heatstroke. Amongst the recognisable costumes which she could see were bunny girls, nurses, a Hannibal Lecter, vicars and a clutch of male Carmen Mirandas—Brazil's own legend—complete with glittery eyeshadow and pyramids of fruit piled high on their heads.

Her lips twitched again. Whatever they were, the costumes had one thing in common: they managed to expose more than they concealed.

'Another glass of wine?' enquired Marco, who was sitting on her other side.

Ellen smiled. He was a cheerful, chunkily built man in his late thirties and he seemed to have appointed himself as her personal waiter.

'Thanks, but I'll have sparkling water this time,' she told him.

'No one minds if you get a little tipsy,' he said, winking at her as he filled her glass.

Ellen laughed. 'No one minds about anything,' she replied as an elderly, cigar-smoking Madonna in an aggressively pointed bra cha-chaed by on his platform heels.

'Only that you should have a good time,' Marco said.

'I am,' she assured him sincerely.

As Ellen had bathed and dressed for the ball, she had wondered whether she might feel a little out of it amongst Jader's long-time friends, but they were a welcoming bunch. She had immediately felt relaxed with them and all four were relaxed with her, drawing her into the conversation and either speaking English or letting her take her time with her Portuguese. Leila and Nilson, who were dressed as an angel and a devil respectively, had once lived in England and were eager to reminisce, while Anna and Marco were warm and fun and marvellously easygoing.

Ellen sneaked another look at her escort. Perhaps it was because she had agreed not to write her article, or due to his taking a break from the pressures of work—or a combination of both—but since the car wash incident Jader had been easygoing too. When they had dined at the *rodizio* the previous evening, and today—no, yesterday, Ellen corrected herself mentally; it was long past midnight now—when he had joined her on the cable car and later driven her up a winding route through the forest to Corcovado, he had been friendly.

She did not doubt that his basic disapproval of her remained, yet Jader was happy to smile, to chat, to make her laugh. Their relationship might be full of contradictions, but—for now—they were no longer at loggerheads.

Ellen gazed down at their clasped hands. Why was his disapproval of her so unshakeable and enduring? she wondered. If he took a long, hard look at the past, surely he must adjust his views and realise that she could not have been the 'soulless little bitch' whom he had imagined?

'How come you let Jader settle for shirt and shorts?' enquired Marco. He indicated his own Al Capone outfit of black shirt, white tie, white trousers and a black trilby with white band. 'Us Italian guys should remind the world of our presence.'

'Italian?' Ellen queried, looking at Jader, who, on hearing his name, had turned towards her.

'Conrado was of Portuguese descent, but my mother's folks came originally from Rome,' he explained.

'Both sets of my grandparents were from Germany,' piped up Anna, who was a strawberry-blonde. Wearing lilac baby-doll pyjamas and with a lilac ribbon tied in her hair, she professed to have come as a Barbie doll, though her plumpness made her look more like a refugee from the Good Ship Lollipop.

Leila grinned across the table. 'I'm half Portuguese, half Syrian.'

'And my ancestry is Spanish with a trace of Brazilian Indian,' said Nilson, whose smooth black hair and chiselled cheekbones gave confirmation to his bloodline.

'How about you, Ellen?' asked Marco.

'Nothing so exotic,' she said, and glanced at Jader. 'I'm one hundred per cent buttoned-up Anglo-Saxon.'

He laughed. 'You're not buttoned up tonight,' he said, crooking an arm around her neck.

Ellen felt the touch of his warm bare arm on her warm bare shoulders. 'No,' she agreed.

She was not buttoned up mentally, she thought, nor in her appearance. After much agonising, she had decided to wear a black satin slip dress which hung straight to the knee and resembled a flapper's dress. She usually wore it over a white T-shirt, but worn alone, and having a dipped neckline with shoestring straps, the dress revealed the smooth width of her shoulders and upper swell of her breasts.

The diamanté headband, hold-up stockings and a pair of strappy black patent, high-heeled sandals completed an outfit which, while it might not be authentic Twenties, was near enough. Besides, the apparel of other guests confirmed what Jader had said: era was unimportant.

'Would you like to dance?' Jader enquired.

Ellen gave an enthusiastic nod. 'Yes, please.'

She had danced with him several times before, and with Marco and Nilson, and with a couple of male friends of the group who had wandered up with their partners to chat, stayed a while, and wandered away again. But the band played to an alluring beat and after a rest and a drink the evening's high-octane energy had gripped again.

Taking her by the hand, Jader led her into the clusters of laughing, writhing bodies. A succession of Latin American rhythms had given way to rock music and they started to bump and grind, to jive and boogie. Raising her arms above her head, Ellen moved around in a circle in front of him.

'You have a delectable *bunda*,' he murmured as she gave a sexy little wriggle of her hips. 'A delectable backside.'

Ellen arched a brow. 'Are you flirting with me?' she enquired.

Jader grinned. 'I thought it was the other way around. No knicker line?' he asked as she circled in front of him again.

'No knickers,' she said.

Clasping an arm around her waist, he drew her near. 'Hussy,' he whispered, into her ear.

Ellen laughed. 'Prude,' she replied.

They danced on, smiling at each other and exchanging the occasional comment. She *was* flirting, Ellen thought as she glanced teasingly at her partner from beneath her lashes, but flirting was fun. They were holding a silent conversation with their eyes, a conversation which spoke of mutual attraction and growing desire. It added a lift to her heart, a kick to her step, an extra buzz to the night.

Caught up in their own private world, Ellen was surprised, and a little disappointed, when the rock music session came to an end. The band leader announced an interval and they returned to their table, where Ellen found Anna and Leila waiting for her.

'We thought we'd go and freshen up,' Anna said, with a smile. 'Want to come along?'

Withdrawing her hand from Jader's, Ellen picked up her jet beaded purse. 'Please.'

Keeping well clear of the pool where several revellers had jumped in—or been pushed in—and were splashing, they made their way to the ladies' room. A tap had been left running, and Ellen held her wrists beneath the cold water and felt herself start to cool down. Drying her hands, she walked through into the carpeted lounge area which, with only a couple of transitory occupants, made a quiet oasis.

Ellen looked at herself in a full-length mirror. When she had been dressing, first her strapless bra had shown in the low back of her dress and so she had shed it. Then she had noticed the spoiling shape of her briefs beneath the black satin and had stepped out of them. It was the first time she had gone without underwear and she started to dither about it—until she had remembered the shop assistant telling her to 'live a little'.

But now perspiration meant that her dress was beginning to cling and the jut of her nipples had become alarmingly noticeable. Sitting down at one of the frill-skirted dressing tables, Ellen renewed her lipstick and combed her hair. At another time and place, the clinging dress and the wantonness of her body would have bothered her. But not tonight.

'Leila and I are so pleased Jader's found himself a girlfriend,' Anna remarked as they came to join her. She smiled. 'Such a nice one, too.'

'Thanks, but I'm not Jader's girlfriend,' Ellen said.

'No?' Anna looked at Leila, who lifted surprised brows. 'But he seems—' she hesitated, thinking how to phrase her English '—so taken with you.'

'He isn't. I'm just—' now it was Ellen's turn to hesitate '—a family friend.'

'Jader mentioned that he'd known you when you were younger and had met your mother,' Leila said, 'but even so we thought the two of you were—' She gave a rueful smile. 'Sorry.'

'That's OK,' Ellen replied.

Sitting at dressing tables on either side of her, the two women started to touch up their make-up and do their hair.

'I wish Jader would find someone,' Leila said, sighing. She was a slender brunette with a swinging bob and big doe eyes. She wore a short white froufrou dress and a pair of increasingly crumpled silver Lurex wings. 'He insists he's in favour of marriage and that he'll get around to it eventually, but his father's experiences appear to have made him cautious.'

'His father's experiences? What do you mean?' Ellen enquired, and frowned, wondering if this might somehow be an indictment of her.

Anna took over the dialogue. 'Although Conrado's first marriage started off happily enough, his wife—Jader's mother—developed a disease of the nervous system when Jader was—oh, eleven or twelve. The illness went into remission from time to time, but from then on until she died around ten years later she was always frail and for the last twelve months she was an invalid. Conrado remained faithful; he was that kind of man,' the blonde declared, and shone an affectionate smile. 'However, unfortunately his wife's poor health meant that she was unable to be a proper partner.'

'He was devoted to her, but over the years their relationship gradually changed from a love match into one of platonic affection,' Leila defined.

'After she passed away, everyone hoped Conrado would find a woman who would brighten up his life and be a good wife. The kind of loving soul mate whom he deserved,' Anna continued, patting a powder puff over her face. 'But along came Yolanda.'

'She didn't brighten up his life?' Ellen enquired.

'In so far as she gave him his second family, yes. But as far as being a good wife, no.'

'We don't believe that Yolanda ever loved him, for himself,' said Leila. 'Her single aim was to have children, and she saw her chance and grabbed him. OK, he was much older, but none of the boys of her own age were ready to settle down.' She sighed. 'It's also doubtful whether Conrado ever loved her.'

Ellen's brow puckered. This was not the idyllically happy marriage which she had imagined. 'But he moved to Rio to please Yolanda,' she protested.

Anna shook her head. 'Conrado moved because he realised that if he insisted on them living in São Paulo she'd spend most of her time up here anyway. Yolanda's an only daughter who was born after her parents had had five sons—'

'A late baby and a spoiled, petulant child,' inserted Leila.

'—and she's suffocatingly close to her family and in particular to her mother.'

'She consults dear mama about every least thing,' Leila derided.

'Conrado realised that when they had kids—and she became pregnant virtually on their wedding night—Yolanda would be bringing them to stay with grandmama at every opportunity and for as long as possible. However, he wanted to be an involved father and play a full part in his children's lives, so he accepted that the best solution—perhaps the only solution—was to set up home here.'

'Conrado and Yolanda had nothing in common apart from their children,' the brunette declared.

Anna nodded. 'She talks endlessly about them, and about her parents and her brothers, but takes no interest in anyone or anything else.' She pulled a face. 'Yolanda must've caught Conrado in a very weak moment.'

'Jader once said something about his father marrying on the rebound,' Leila remarked, 'though from whom no one knows. Conrado was a private person who kept any romantic activities to himself.'

'Whether it was on the rebound or not, he couldn't have been thinking straight when he married Yolanda,' Anna declared.

No, he was thinking about my mother, Ellen said silently.

'Where did they meet?' she asked.

'At the wedding of one of Yolanda's brothers. Conrado had been invited because he was a business associate of the bride's father.'

Pushing back her chair, Leila stood up. 'The men'll be wondering what's happened to us,' she said, 'so we'd better be getting back.'

When they returned, the lights which encircled the dance-floor had dimmed and the band were playing a slow, smoochy number. As Ellen approached the table, Jader looked at her, flicked his gaze towards the dance-floor and, when she nodded, rose to his feet. In silence, he navigated her through to a space and drew her into his arms. As the sound of a smoky, swooning saxophone rose in the night, Ellen wrapped her arms around his neck. The music was seductive, the press of his body was seductive. There was little room for steps, and they swayed slowly together.

As the band played on, Jader rubbed his cheek against her hair. He pulled her closer so that her breasts were against his chest and her hips met his pelvis. Ellen's breath caught in her throat. His arousal was hard against her and she felt a fierce tingle in her loins which marked her response. The erotic temperature between them was soaring, making her blood hum and her breasts feel heavy and tender.

Jader looked down at her. 'Ellen,' he said. It was the first time he had spoken and he seemed to roll her name around his mouth as if tasting a priceless brandy. 'Ellen,' he repeated softly, and lowered his head.

His lips opened on hers, and as his tongue thrust into the moist recesses of her mouth in a violently sexual kiss the humming blood began to roar in her head. Any pretence at dancing ceased and they stood still in the midst of the crowd, pressed together. The kiss went on and on, growing in intensity until, as if he feared it might get out of control—as if he feared *he* might lose control—Jader drew back.

'How about we get out of here and go home to bed?' he said.

Ellen looked at him. Her heart seemed to have gone into free fall and her mind was dazed, but she knew exactly what he meant—it was there in the silent but unerring language of eye contact. She drew in a breath. Although she had dallied with the idea of a holiday romance, up until now she had always been cautious with her emotions and she would be breaking her rules—but why *shouldn't* she have a fling?

Rising up on tiptoe, Ellen kissed his cheek. 'Let's,' she said.

CHAPTER FIVE

As THEY made hasty farewells to his surprised yet smiling friends, and throughout the journey home—which did not take long because the night roads were quiet and Jader drove at speed—Ellen had no doubts. Not one. Nor in the lift from the basement car park, when he hauled her into his arms and kissed her again. But, as the lift stopped, the doors slid apart and he released her, second thoughts arrived. All of a sudden she was startlingly aware of what she had agreed to and stricken with the instinctive knowledge that in making love she would be wading into dangerous emotional waters.

Though she had not actually agreed to anything, Ellen argued with herself as Jader took the key which she had kept in her purse and unlocked the door of the apartment. She walked ahead of him into the hall. Their going to bed together was not compulsory, or even a foregone conclusion. Was it? Yes. No. Her mind see-sawed. Well, maybe. Yet even if she had been momentarily taken hostage by her hormones she could escape. Jader might state his displeasure at her capriciousness in no uncertain terms, but he would not force her into anything against her will. So, what should she say?

Pulling off the diamanté headband, Ellen ruffled a hand through her hair. Should she claim she had believed he had straightforwardly meant for them to come back and go to their separate beds? Or plead a sudden headache? Or should she act flip and say, Oops! Sorry, buster—making love does not seem like such a brilliant idea after all?

'Did you notice that Michael Jackson look-alike?' was what Ellen did say.

Jader closed the door behind them. 'Excuse me?'

'The young guy dressed up like Michael Jackson—' she shone a bright smile '—with the black trilby and the single glove. And the black leather, silver-studded jacket and the curl that dangled in front of his eyes.'

'I noticed him,' he said, frowning at what she knew must seem an unusual sudden interest.

'When he was dancing he did the moonwalk; I don't know if you noticed that too,' Ellen rattled on, 'but he was terrific. I've always wished I could moonwalk.'

She was standing to one side of the hallway and Jader placed his hands flat on the wall on either side of her head. 'Have you?' he said, leaning over her.

'Yes.' Ellen smiled another bright smile. She could not decide which get-out to use and until she did she needed to keep on talking. She would have liked to keep moving too, she thought, casting a wistful glance towards her bedroom door, but he had effectively caged her in. 'To be able to do Irish dancing is something else I've always fancied,' she continued. 'Have you seen it? How they kick their legs from the knees and—'

Jader leaned closer. 'Shut up,' he said, and he kissed her.

Ellen had no chance to resist, though, as his mouth pressed warm and soft on hers, she could not resist. Her lips parted at the subtle need inherent in his and as his tongue came between them an elemental heat burst into flame inside her. It burned away her doubts and reduced the nervousness to cinders. Opening her fingers, Ellen let the purse and headband tumble to the floor. Her hand was placed at his waist. She wanted them to make love. She wanted to give him the gift of her body. She had never wanted anything so intensely in all her life.

As if sensing the change of heart and her need, Jader stood up straight. He drew her away from the wall, wound an arm around her and, with his other hand, began to stroke a thumbtip across the sensitive hollow behind her ear. He kissed her again, tasting and tenderly savouring, then his mouth moved to explore the column of her throat and the line of her shoulders.

'Black, slippery, sensual,' Jader murmured, sliding a hand slowly over one firm breast and down across her stomach to stop on her hip.

Ellen stirred beneath his touch. Although only a fragile layer of satin was separating his hand from her body, she needed to be naked. She longed to feel the stroke of his fingers on her naked flesh. Undress me, she implored silently and telepathy—or perhaps equal need?—existed, for Jader took hold of the skirt of her dress and drew it up. He slithered the black satin up over her waist, her breasts, her head and dropped it in a soft, rippled pool of jet on the white marble floor. All Ellen wore now were the fishnet stockings with their lacy tops and her strappy high-heeled sandals.

Jader took a step back. The hall was lit by the golden glow from a table lamp which sat on a chest and, for a moment, he gazed at her through the muted light, then his eyes started to roam over her. Over her tumbled fair head, over her uptilted breasts with their blatantly pointed nipples centred in wine-red aureoles, over the smooth plane of her stomach and to the intimate blonde triangle which spread at her groin. Ellen stood straight and silent. A few days ago she might have rushed to shield herself from his gaze in the kitchen, but tonight she felt proud to be a shapely, alluring woman and proud to be desired.

As his visual homage ended, Jader raised his head and stepped nearer. He stroked his hands down her sides.

'A satin dress and a body made of satin,' he said huskily, and, lifting his arms, he started to slowly circle the heel of his hands across the tips of her breasts.

Ellen drew in a sharp breath. She clenched her teeth and arched her back. The rubbing of his smooth, hard flesh against the sensitive peaks was exquisite. Agony and bliss. Heaven and delicious hell. Her eyelids lowered. Her breathing quickened. A bitter-sweet ache had begun to gnaw between her thighs when she felt his long fingers on her breasts. Jader was rolling, caressing, pinching the wine-dark nubs.

Ellen opened her eyes. The ache was howling inside her. 'Jader,' she said, in a voice which turned his name into a plea, and, reaching out, she started to pull at the buttons on his shirt.

He placed a calming hand over her scurrying fingers and rested his forehead against hers.

'I'm sweaty,' he said hoarsely, and, as if on cue, a bead of perspiration trickled down his jaw. 'Heaven knows, I don't want to stop us now, but I really need to shower.' He pulled back to smile. 'How about showering with me?'

Ellen nodded. 'But first I need to pin up my hair,' she decided, dipping down to retrieve her purse.

'I'll meet you in my shower in one minute.' As she turned away, Jader slapped her lightly on the rear. 'Don't go changing your mind,' he commanded.

She looked back at him over her shoulder. 'There's no chance,' Ellen said, smiling, and with a tip-tap of heels she disappeared.

In her bedroom, she twisted her hair into a burnished

blonde knot which she pinned on the top of her head. Even
if she managed to avoid standing beneath the full rush of
the shower her hair was bound to get a little wet, but she
refused to wear a shower cap!

After shedding stockings and her sandals, Ellen made
her way barefoot through Jader's bedroom to the cream-
tiled bathroom. In the doorway, she paused. He had
stripped off his clothes and was standing beneath the water
in the glass cubicle, soaping himself. Her heart began to
pound. The fellow student at university and the co-
journalist who had been her previous lovers were pale of
skin, but Jader was golden. Golden and well built and
strong.

She watched the rhythmic foaming of his chest, saw
flattened streaks of dark hair when he lifted an arm to rub
at his armpit, felt her pounding heart beat faster as he
lathered a muscled thigh. Ellen stood entranced. He was
the magnificent male animal which she had imagined.

As he completed his soaping, Jader glanced up and saw
her. 'Come,' he said, opening the shower door, and Ellen
stepped in inside.

In instant fusion, they started kissing again and, as their
half-open mouths yearningly nibbled and tasted, he began
to lather her. Using smooth milled soap with a lavendar
fragrance, Jader massaged the tablet over her shoulders,
around and across her back and down to the roundness of
her rump. In time, he returned to her shoulders and worked
down to her breasts. Lingeringly, he soaped the high
curves, feeling their smooth undersides, the hardened nipples, the full shape.

As they kissed, Jader captured her cushiony lower lip
between his teeth and gently bit.

'Such a seductive mouth. Ever since I saw you at the
airport, I've wanted to do that,' he told her. His lathering

continued, over her stomach and down to her thighs. 'And since that very first sight I've been longing to make love to you. I fought it, but I've seemed unable to stop touching you. You've been driving me mad,' he complained.

As the soap frothed amongst the tangle of wet curls and his fingers dipped between her legs, Ellen pressed instinctively against his hand.

'Likewise,' she said chokily.

As if growing abruptly impatient, Jader dropped the soap in the tray and, standing beneath the jet, rinsed himself clean. He moved them around.

'Your turn,' he said, and, keeping her head as clear of the spray as she could, Ellen sluiced herself down.

Jader switched off the water. He had seemed eager to quit the shower, but now he stepped closer and his thigh pushed between hers. Ellen quivered. The velvet length of his arousal was pressed hard against her belly and she could feel the hairy roughness of his thigh against the intimate petals of her flesh.

As though kissing her were a drug without which he would die, Jader began to kiss her again. He kissed her mouth, her shoulders, her gleaming breasts. And as he kissed his hands stroked urgently over her wet-slicked body.

'Better than the car wash?' he murmured, his mouth taking on a humorous curve as he kissed her nipples.

Ellen smiled and dragged in a breath. The lapping of his tongue was sending spears of sensation shooting through her, awakening every nerve to the erotic torture.

'Much better,' she told him.

She moved against his intruding thigh, tentatively at first, but her hips gaining a compulsive rhythm. With his mouth, his tongue, his fingers, Jader seemed to be unleashing a primitive part of her, releasing a passion which dizzied her head and flooded from every pore. As his fingers replaced his mouth and he rolled her nipple between a thumb and a finger, a spasm pierced through her. It tweaked at her swollen breasts and sped down to sting in that most secret part of her.

'Make love to me,' Ellen said.

Jader frowned. 'Here?'

'Yes. Now,' she begged, desperate for the fulfilment which she craved and unable to wait a moment longer.

He hesitated, looked down, then stepped her onto the broad tiled ledge which edged the cubicle. Now their heights were more even and their bodies met on a closer equivalent level. Easing her thighs apart, he slid into her. Ellen gasped.

'So hot, so ready,' Jader muttered.

Her hands curled around his shoulders and with her fingers biting in Ellen clung, feeling the power of him deep inside her. They seemed to be bolted together at the pelvis, when Jader drew back and thrust again. She murmured, absorbing his maleness and his heat. Her head was spinning when he moved a second time and, as a shudder racked through his body, they cried out together.

Ellen sagged against him, her head on his shoulder. Her breathing was quick and erratic, and it took a minute or two before she could manage to speak.

'What happened?' she said.

Jader grinned. 'You told me to make love to you, so I did. It was a darn sight quicker than I expected, but at least it means that we can now take our time in bed.' Abruptly, his brow furrowed and he swore. 'We should've taken precautions. Dammit, I *always* take precautions.'

'Don't worry,' Ellen told him. 'I'm on the Pill.'

He hissed out a breath. 'Thank you,' he said, and turned on the water again.

When they had washed themselves, Jader stepped out of the cubicle. 'I'll dry you and afterwards you dry me,' he said, lifting a thick white bath towel from the rail.

Although Jader's drying began in a serious, businesslike manner, the eroticism of him towelling her naked body proved too much and desire quickly took control. They started to kiss and caress, one kiss leading to another, this caress inspiring the next. The towelling became intermittent, though body heat was drying her now, and for endless pleasurable minutes they were wrapped around each other. When he finally stood back, Ellen was light-headed and panting.

'Let's do me together,' Jader said. 'It'll be quicker.'

She nodded. Whilst she would have been happy to play things his way, Ellen could not help feeling secretly relieved that on this, their first time together, she was not expected to dry the most private parts of him.

The towelling soon done, Jader led her back into his bedroom, which was shadowy with the first pearly light of dawn.

'Let me,' he requested, when Ellen reached up to unfasten her hair.

With his dark eyes solemn and the pink tip of his tongue showing between his lips in concentration, Jader withdrew the pins and watched as the skeins of wheat-blonde hair fell heavily around her shoulders. He touched a swirling strand.

'Body of satin and hair like golden silk,' he murmured.

Drawing back the covers, Jader pulled her down with him onto the bed. He kissed her, cupping and cradling her breasts, and, moving down beside her, drew her nipple into his mouth. He sucked hungrily on the eager peak.

'Harder,' Ellen appealed, and arched her spine, straining

closer as she flagrantly flaunted her need. 'Oh, yes,' she breathed.

Jader feasted on her nipple and when it felt hot and deliciously sore he transferred his mouth to her other breast. Again he suckled her. For countless time, Ellen abandoned herself to the shimmering waves of pleasure and when Jader eventually lay back on the pillow she bent over him. Now it was her turn to please him. With her hair trailing over his chest, she kissed his flat brown nipples and dragged her breasts across their alien hardness, sensually teasing him. Jader shuddered, and when she looked at him she saw a dark stain of colour on his skin. Ellen smiled. She had not realised she would have such a powerful effect on him—and it thrilled her.

Jader drew in a deep breath. 'I wondered if you might be like this,' he said.

'Like what?' Ellen asked.

'Outwardly appear so demure and yet be so passionate in bed.' She felt him smile. 'It's an erotic combination.'

Lifting herself up on one elbow, Ellen slowly dragged her fingers down his chest and over the flatness of his belly to his thighs. As her fingers reached the dynamic thrust of his manhood, Jader groaned. Made brave by his desire, she curled her fingers around the pulsing muscle and bent her head.

'That is unbearable,' he said raggedly.

Ellen touched him again with her tongue, inhaling his muskiness. 'I know,' she replied.

'I want you now,' Jader said, in a low, driven voice, and steered her back down onto the bed.

Looming over her like a dark shadow, he bent and she felt his rasping tongue at the core of her, licking over the saturated wings of her sex. Ellen trembled. She had never experienced such intensity of arousal before. Jader straddled her and as he slid into her she lifted her pelvis to meet him. A shudder galvanised his body and he started to move in deep, hard thrusts. Ellen adapted herself to his special rhythm and, as a powerful convulsion gripped her, breathed in a rush of air. She could feel herself lifting, whirling, spinning. She was on the brink—that delicious, fraught, fervent brink of ecstasy. Ellen started to tumble, to fall.

'Jader,' she gasped.

'Yes,' he said, his voice harsh and guttural, and, in a climactic mingling of emotions, bodies, essences, they gave themselves to each other.

Ellen awoke slowly. She stretched. Her body felt deliciously used and sated with love. She opened her eyes. The sun shone bright behind the curtains and when she squinted at the clock which sat on the bedside table she saw that it was past two o'clock. Turning over carefully so that she did not disturb him, she looked at Jader who lay fast asleep beside her. His dark hair was rumpled, his long lashes were spread on his cheeks and his chest softly rose and fell. Ellen smiled. He looked younger when he was asleep, and boyishly defenceless.

Reaching out, she gently lifted a strand of dark hair from his brow. Jader was neither defenceless nor a boy; he was a man—with a man's strengths and desires. She was grateful that he had been experienced in lovemaking, Ellen mused, for his stroking fingers had contained a knowledge, an expertise which had lifted her to heights of sensuality that she had never known existed. Jader had been everything expected of a Latin lover—erotic, demanding, caring, ardent. He was the perfect lover. She sighed. And now the differences of the past could be forgotten and the future held so much potential.

Ellen eyed the clock again. The day was passing, so should she sidle up closer and gently wake him with kisses? A grin tweaked her mouth. And they could make love again. Though perhaps it would be kinder to let him sleep on? His workload was heavy and a lie-in must be beneficial.

Ellen was regretfully deciding that his need for rest came before her desire, when the telephone on the bedside table pealed out. Startled, she jumped, and felt Jader stir beside her. However, his eyes did not open, so when the phone started to ring a second time she stretched out an arm and picked it up.

'*Boa tarde,*' Ellen said, speaking in a hushed voice and holding the receiver close to her ear.

There was silence at the other end of the line, then a woman's voice asked, in Portuguese, who was speaking.

'My name is Ellen Blanchard and I am a friend of Mr de Sa Moreira's,' she replied, answering softly in the same language. 'Who is calling?'

'This is Yolanda.'

'Yolanda?' Ellen echoed, her voice lifting in surprise.

She was thinking up how to say 'I'm sorry, but Mr de Sa Moreira is not available right now', when the mattress gave a sudden lurch, a muscled arm reached over and Jader commandeered the telephone.

'*Boa tarde,*' he said, and placed a large hand over the mouthpiece. 'I'll take it,' he told her, sitting up and hooking the cord behind her pillow.

Not wishing to lie there and awkwardly listen in, Ellen pushed back the sheet. 'I'll get up,' she said, and sped off to her own room.

Ellen washed and dressed and brushed her hair, then, since there were still sounds of Jader speaking on the telephone, went through to the kitchen. She had prepared a grapefruit half for herself, made wholemeal toast for him, and was percolating the coffee when he came in. She looked at him. His slicked-back, damp dark hair indicated that he had showered and he wore a checked short-sleeved shirt, jeans and sneakers. Ellen felt a lurch of disappointment. She had been wondering whether—hoping that—the still naked Jader might insist on undressing her and them going back to bed, but obviously lovemaking was not a plan.

'Coffee?' she asked.

'Please,' Jader replied, pulling out a chair and sitting down at the pine table.

Ellen poured cups for them both, then sat down opposite. She had expected him to kiss her, but a kiss did not appear to feature in his plans either. Indeed, he looked solemn and was frowning.

'Is there a problem?' she enquired.

Jader looked up. 'Excuse me?' he said sharply.

'With Yolanda.'

'Oh…yes. Julia's developed a cough and she's wondering whether to call in the doctor.'

'Yolanda rang to ask you that?' Ellen protested, digging into her grapefruit.

He nodded. 'Normally she'd ring her mother or one of her brothers, but her parents are taking a vacation in the States and apparently her brothers aren't answering their phones and must be out.' He scowled. 'So I'm the next on her list. Yolanda went on and on and on, but she doesn't need my advice because she'll bring in the doctor anyway. She just needs to be in the spotlight and to make a fuss.' He took a mouthful of coffee. 'She knew I was staying in Rio over the holiday, but she was surprised when a woman answered the telephone.'

Ellen shot him a look. She had heard criticism in his

voice. 'I answered it because you were asleep,' she said, 'and I wanted to stop the ringing from waking you.'

'OK, but you gave Yolanda your name—your full name.' Jader put down his cup. 'She didn't comment on it just now, but she could easily make the connection and realise you must be related to Vivienne.'

Ellen chewed at the grapefruit. He might have been the perfect lover in the early hours of the morning, but the afternoon had brought a distinct change of mood.

'So?' she enquired.

'So Yolanda's going to wonder what on earth you're doing here,' he said, 'and if it dawns on her that Conrado could've had something to do with your visit she may not be too pleased. I ought to explain that my stepmother expects the world to revolve around *her* and isn't averse to throwing the odd tantrum,' Jader went on tersely, 'which could occur should she realise Vivienne was more than a business associate. And I've enough to cope with right now without her appearing on my doorstep to demand answers to questions and scream belated abuse.'

He reached for a slice of toast. 'I think it'd be best if you leave Rio on Thursday straight after the Carnival, as was originally planned.'

'But I'll be moving out of your apartment then anyway, so your stepmother's not going to know that I'm still around,' Ellen pointed out.

Jader spread butter on his toast. 'I'd feel easier if you flew home.'

She put down her spoon. An increasing tightness in her throat made it impossible for her to eat another segment of fruit. She had believed their lovemaking had meant something to him, that now *she* meant something, Ellen thought and gave a harsh inner laugh. What a major-league prize-winning bozo! Jader did not give a damn about her.

They might have shared a wonderful night of love, but her oh, so reluctant host was back to being disapproving again.

'I bet you would. I bet you'd feel much easier, but, tough luck, I'm staying!' Ellen announced.

His dark brows came down. 'Look, if Yolanda—'

'Forget Yolanda. She doesn't feature in this,' she snapped. 'It's *you* who doesn't want me around—and never did. That's why you held off from inviting me until the last minute.' Ellen's blue eyes glittered. To realise she remained an unwelcome guest was a crushing blow, but she refused to curl up into a pathetic little ball and rock. 'Isn't it?' she demanded.

Jader heaved a noisy sigh. 'In part,' he admitted.

'The most part.'

'OK, OK,' he said impatiently, 'but when I read my father's letter the idea of inviting you threw me. I'd never expected it and I didn't know what I felt about it and I continually delayed making a decision. However, in the end I kept faith with his wishes—' he moved his shoulders '—and here you are.'

'Your better feelings came briefly to the fore, but now you can't wait to get rid of me. It figures,' Ellen said, in a brittle voice. 'As I recall, the last time we met back in London you told me that if you ever saw me again it'd be too soon.'

Jader frowned. 'I lost my temper and went a little… wild.'

'You went *far* too wild,' she retorted.

'Maybe, but I was young and I was reacting to a situation, a traumatic situation—' his brown eyes clashed with hers '—which *you'd* created. Have you any idea how my father felt when you persuaded Vivienne to dump him? When he returned to our hotel, he was devastated, broken! He looked like he'd aged ten years. It'd taken him a long time after my mother died before he would even consider a new relationship and then the women he dated never really appealed, until he met Vivienne. He fell for her completely.'

'I know,' Ellen said, though Jader did not seem to hear.

'After all the sad years, it was as if his life had started anew and he went around smiling, singing. I'd never seen my father so happy. When I asked him the reason, he confessed that he'd met a beautiful English woman and, as the months passed, he became noticeably more and more enamoured. More content. On our flight to London, he told me he intended asking Vivienne to be his wife and spoke of the pleasurable marriage which he anticipated.' Jader shot her a stony look. 'Only he married Yolanda.'

'You blame me?' she said, though it was more of a statement than a question.

'Conrado would never've looked at her twice in the normal way of things, but at the time they met he was distracted, depressed, raw with misery. Vivienne had been the great love of his life—'

'He loved her more than your mother?' Ellen interrupted.

'I believe so; I believe it was a great love, the kind which occurs once in a lifetime—if you're lucky. I also believe Vivienne loved him too, and they would've been so—' Jader slammed is fist down on the table, making the crockery jump '— *right* together. They were of a similar age and had similar interests; she made him laugh. Vivienne's well read, well travelled and speaks—how many languages?'

'Four.'

'OK, Yolanda's learned English, but that was only because Conrado insisted the kids should speak it and, when the time comes, she wants to be able to help them with their lessons. I've never known her read anything more than a women's magazine, and mention a country like Bulgaria and she looks blank.

'Vivienne would've been equally at ease whether at a barbecue with my father's friends,' he went on, 'or dining in a presidential palace. She was—is—a sophisticated and gracious lady. Whereas Yolanda—' Jader gave a humourless laugh. 'Let's just say that although she comes from Rio she's a small-town girl with a small-town mind who expects to have her own way.'

Ellen looked at him across the table. Now she understood why, ten years after the denouement of his father's relationship with her mother, he still disapproved of her. The unfortunate second marriage had been a constant reminder of her supposedly selfish manipulation; it had stoked his hostility and kept it alive.

'You didn't tell Conrado you felt Yolanda was not a good choice?' she enquired.

'I tried,' Jader said tersely, 'but he was so in need of someone—anyone—to help divert him from his pain and offer what seemed like hope that he wouldn't listen. However, it didn't take him long to realise he'd made a dreadful mistake. When they married, my father decided to pack in work because the iron ore business no longer held any interest for him,' he continued. 'Though,' he said pungently, 'after losing Vivienne, few things did. But a couple of months alone with Yolanda had him climbing the walls and because he was desperate for an escape he came up with the idea of the car company.'

'And he started it without thinking it through properly,' Ellen said.

'Yes. Conrado remained depressed and distracted—the loss of Vivienne was a constant sorrow to the day he died;

the loss of her to him was as if *she* had died,' Jader stated, 'and he went in blindly.'

'That's my fault too? Of course it is,' she said, not needing his reply. She speared him with a look. 'You could also say that Conrado's second family is my fault, but he loved his children.'

'True. They meant so much to him. Both he and Yolanda were besotted parents and when all of them were together the kids made their marriage palatable. Just,' Jader rasped.

Ellen lifted her spoon, eyed the grapefruit, and put the spoon down again. 'I didn't persuade my mother to dump Conrado,' she said slowly.

He gave a curt laugh. 'Play it straight,' he derided. 'Even if you were only sixteen, you were the stronger-minded of the two of you.'

'Maybe, though—'

'It was you who decided the relationship must end. Wasn't it?' Jader demanded.

Ellen hesitated. 'Well, yes, I suppose—'

'I knew it,' he scythed. 'Guilty as charged. You'd realised Conrado was planning to propose, but you didn't fancy the idea of upping sticks and coming to live in Brazil.'

She looked at him in surprise. 'You think that's what I said that morning?'

'I believe it's a possibility, though my father always refused point-blank to explain so all I have are theories.' Jader took a drink of coffee, grimacing when he discovered it had gone cold. 'However, it seems viable.'

'To you maybe, but not to me,' Ellen said. 'Why would visiting Rio have always been my dream if I'd had an aversion to Brazil?'

'Coming for a holiday is not the same as living in a

country,' he said brusquely, 'but I could've got it wrong.'
He rubbed at his jaw with impatient fingers. 'Maybe you
thought that if Vivienne married my father she'd be over
here while you were left at home to complete your education and you didn't want to be parted from her?'

'We were parted for years when I was a child,' she
pointed out.

'Which could be all the more reason why you objected
to being parted as a teenager. Why you wanted to have
your mother all to yourself and not share her with Conrado,' he declared, though he frowned as if doubting the
credibility of that theory. 'But these are just theories, so
why don't we stop pussyfooting around?' His dark eyes
nailed themselves onto hers. 'Why don't you tell me the
truth?'

Ellen felt a sudden moment of panic. She had more or
less talked herself into this corner, but how did she get out
of it? She might be maintaining Conrado's silence out of
respect for him and yet, if she was honest, she had also
decided to keep quiet for herself. She did not want to tell
Jader the truth, because the truth hurt. It also tainted. And
even if their lovemaking had been a one-night stand and
he was eager to get rid of her at the first possible moment
she could not bear to be tainted in his eyes.

'Both my theories are wrong,' Jader said, when she remained silent.

Ellen frowned. His statement was so certain, there
seemed no point in denying it and attempting to lie.
Though, like his father, he would never be fobbed off with
lies.

'They are,' she agreed.

'And?' he prompted.

'You accepted that Conrado didn't want to tell you the

truth, so can't you accept that I prefer to remain silent too?' Ellen entreated.

Jader gave her a long, unhinging stare, then he shook his head. 'No.'

'But why not?' she appealed.

'Because I loved Conrado more than anyone else on earth and I saw what you did to him. He'd gone through all kinds of hell with my mother, and when he had happiness within his grasp you snatched it away. He never spoke ill of you,' Jader said, when she started to protest. 'Amazingly, he continued to be fond of—' his lip curled '—sweet little Ellie, who apparently couldn't help herself.'

'You don't think maybe I really couldn't help myself and that Conrado had sound reasons for remaining fond?' Ellen demanded.

'Perhaps, but I need you to explain. And unless you do—' Jader moved his shoulders.

Torn between angst and anger, she gazed at him. 'You're very judgemental,' she said. 'Have you never wondered why your father left me the shares? Hasn't it occurred to you that he wouldn't have done so if he'd believed I'd snatched away his happiness *on purpose*?'

'It has,' he replied. 'However, it's also occurred to me that he may have wanted to leave something to Vivienne as an expression of his eternal love for her, but, fearing it could arouse Yolanda's suspicions and cause trouble, decided it would be more discreet to leave the shares to you, her daughter.'

'And my mother would understand his message?'

Jader nodded. 'Or maybe he suffered a mental lapse. Like I said, he never properly recovered from losing Vivienne and could often be distracted.'

'But whatever the reason for Conrado gifting me the

shares you're hell-bent on blaming me for his unhappiness?' Ellen demanded.

His brown eyes were cool and certain. 'If you're hell-bent on not telling me what you said to my father which made him so unhappy—yes.'

Her insides hollowed. Her heart bled. Life was full of tough choices, yet whichever choice she made she was trapped. Doomed to Jader's continuing antagonism if she remained silent, doomed if she spoke.

'What are you so ashamed of?' Jader enquired. 'All right, you were only sixteen and adolescence isn't known for its wisdom and with hindsight you probably regret breaking up the relationship—'

'I don't,' Ellen said.

His lean face darkened. 'No?'

'No. My reasons were valid then and they're valid now.'

Jader looked at her, then, rising to his feet, he pushed back his chair. 'I'm going for a jog,' he said, and a moment later the front door banged shut.

Resting her elbows on the table, Ellen sank her head into her hands. Why, after making love to her with such ardour and tenderness, must Jader reject her now? she thought wretchedly. Why did she have to pay the price for her mother's past? She swallowed a sob. Whatever theory Jader might come up with next, he would never come up with anything which approached the truth. Yet perhaps if she told him the truth he would be sympathetic? Ellen shook her head. This was wishful thinking. Past experience had taught her a harsh lesson about the value of silence.

Ellen's thoughts returned to Jader and their lovemaking. Whilst she had been stricken with sudden doubts when they had arrived back at the apartment, she could feel no retrospective regret. Their night together had shown her how wonderful passion could be and how she possessed the power to inspire ecstasy. She would always remember it—and feel privileged. Ellen swallowed hard. She would also always curse the deities for allowing her only one night.

Rising, she tipped away her cup of cold coffee. If only she could pack her bags and move to other accommodation today, Ellen thought wistfully. Her host would, she knew, preserve the basic courtesies over the next few days and yet living in close contact with him was destined to be painful. Perhaps it would be easier to depart Rio on Thursday, as planned?

Ellen's chin lifted. No, she wanted to write about the city and take photographs, so she would stay. She might not be the mistress of her fate, but she was a survivor. And if her continued presence in town irritated Jader and made her woefully jumpy—so be it!

CHAPTER SIX

JAZZY in boaters, scarlet jackets and scarlet and gold striped trousers, the band marched forward with a syncopated stride. Ellen raised her camera and, as the sweet sound of trumpets rocketed through the air, focused on a baton-carrying girl with glitter-dusted shoulders and a gold-plumed headdress. Another image was captured, yet this was one occasion when she would far rather look and absorb than bother with photographs.

Lowering her camera, Ellen grinned. The guide books and TV glimpses had been no preparation for the reality of Rio's Carnival parade, which was larger, louder and more overwhelmingly spectacular than she had ever imagined.

It was the next evening and she and Jader were sitting in a stand at the Sambadromo stadium, watching the samba schools go by. Comprising around three thousand people and taking roughly three-quarters of an hour to move down the Passarela do Samba avenue, each school seemed to jump with greater energy and be on an increasingly ambitious scale than the last. But competition to win the coveted 'World Cup' of the Carnival was intense.

'They take their themes from Brazilian culture,' Jader said, beside her, and added, 'Though, as you'll have realised, the interpretation can be loose.'

'Poetic licence run wild,' Ellen remarked, in wry amusement.

Thus far, the procession had included courts of spangled kings and bejewelled queens; platoons of women in the flowing white dresses of Bahia, a Brazilian province, all twirling magically together; a homage to the Hollywood greats which had featured jerky-caned Charlie Chaplins and platinum-wigged Mae Wests; and now they were being entertained by scenes from the Amazonian forest.

Gigantic floats bearing papier-mâché palm trees, fountains of perfumed water and serpents which breathed real fire were being drawn past and, because as well as being marvellous fun the parade was also frankly erotic, each float was topped with beautiful, dignified, bare-breasted girls.

Jader had explained how many of the participants came from the *favelas*, the hillside shanty towns at the back of Rio, Ellen recalled as she snapped again. They were some of the poorest people on earth and this was the one time in the year when they could don fine trappings and 'act rich'. Yet, even if they were soon destined to return to hardscrabble, the Carnival throbbed with a celebration of life.

Jader. Ellen darted a look sideways. No matter how fascinating the cavalcade was below, a part of her remained forever alert to him. Alert to the litheness of his body in a tan and black short-sleeved shirt and black trousers, alert to the occasional brush of his thigh or arm against hers when he moved, alert to his aloofness. A chill touched her heart. Jader's manner was now polite, but formal. He might not be about to restart the battle and attack with all guns firing, yet his stiff formality made it clear that he was counting the days until she exited his apartment—and until she left Brazil.

Ellen picked at a fingernail. She had not arrived in the country expecting him to declare her the greatest thing since sliced beets, she thought tensely; all she had wanted was for them to be friends. But even friendship was taboo.

Her melancholy was ended by a tribe of dancers who, with a great whoop of vitality, leapt in front of the stand. Both male and female, young and old, they wore grass skirts and necklaces of multi-coloured baubles, and all were dancing in time. As feet moved fast, hands clapped to the rhythm of the drums, and children dressed as baby leopards sprang recurring somersaults, Ellen felt a lump form in her throat. Such zest, such joy stirred the emotions.

'I could watch all the schools which are appearing to-night,' she declared.

'There are fifteen, which means the show goes on till dawn, but if I should expire from hunger in the meantime, so what?' Jader said pithily, then he smiled. 'We did agree we'd leave at eleven to go and eat, and come back later, but it's almost eleven forty-five.' He raised his brows in a woebegone look. 'And I'm starving!'

Ellen relaxed a little. Her escort's smile had been the first real smile all day and his look was the first jokey gesture—though a person would need to be made of stone not to be affected by the huge affability of the Carnival. Her thoughts tripped. Jader was not made of stone. He was made of sinew and muscle and rich red blood—as she knew to her cost.

'I just wanted to see another school,' she protested, smiling back at him, 'and I have. So we can go now, right this minute.'

'You're sure?' Jader enquired, in dry disbelief, but he too had spotted the battery of mechanical road sweepers which were poised to charge in and administer a brisk wash and brush-up after the present school departed and before the next one arrived. 'You are sure,' he said.

By the time they had made their way down the stand to

ground level, the tail-end of the samba school was disappearing into the distance and the march of the sweepers had begun.

'After you,' Jader said, guiding Ellen ahead of him so that they could make their way single file through the throng of people who had crowded onto the sides of the road.

Because they would be dining at a restaurant half an hour's journey down the coast from Rio—which Jader had said, in his continued yet somewhat strained role of perfect host, should be less frenetic than eating in the city—they had come in the convertible. And, as parking was notoriously difficult on parade evenings, he had arranged to leave the car in the office garage of a business associate which was a few blocks away.

'*Senhor! Senhor!*' a voice suddenly called as they were walking along.

Glancing across the road, Ellen saw a small rotund black woman jumping up and down amidst the crowd and waving madly. She had lustrous bobbing ringlets, wore a bright yellow kaftan and she appeared to be waving at them.

'*Senhor de Sa Moreira,*' the woman cried, confirming the impression.

Ellen waited for Jader to respond and when she heard no sound of acknowledgement she glanced back. He was walking along behind her with his eyes riveted on her backside, seemingly in a trance. She smiled drily. With its nudity and hedonism, the Carnival had created a sexual undercurrent and he had been affected. Ellen gave her hips a rebellious little twitch. The straw-coloured silk jersey skirt which she wore with a matching top did have a tendency to cling.

'You've been recognised,' she said.

Startled, Jader looked up. 'I beg your pardon?' he asked, and frowned when he realised she had caught him out.

'Across the road,' Ellen told him, indicating the waving woman.

Jader smiled and waved back. 'It's Teresa, the maid who looks after my apartment,' he explained when, after proudly identifying her boss to the group of women she was with—which caused some visible oohing and ahhing—the greeter started off across the road towards them. 'You remember I said how one of her daughters was a dancer with the first samba school? Teresa must've stayed on to assess the opposition.'

With a merry torrent of words, the woman arrived. Though Ellen could not manage a complete translation, she did get the general gist, which was that his maid was delighted to meet Senhor de Sa Moreira, had he seen her daughter, and could this be—she smiled a broad, gold-toothed smile at Ellen—the visitor who was vacationing at his apartment?

In a courteous reply, Jader declared equal pleasure at the meeting. Yes, he had seen the samba school, which must be in line for a prize, though, as he only knew her daughter from a photograph, he had regrettably failed to pick her out. And, with a fractional stiffening of his stance, he confirmed that Ellen was his guest.

Clasping hold of her hand, Teresa pumped it up and down. ''Ello, 'ello,' she said. 'It is good meet you.'

She had spoken in fractured English, but, reverting to her mother tongue, she brandished a camera which she carried and declared that she required a photograph of the two of them together.

'I don't think—' Jader started to protest, but Teresa refused to listen.

Whether she was naturally vivacious or on a high from

seeing her daughter, or excited at unexpectedly coming across her boss, Ellen did not know, but the woman proved unstoppable and unbeatable. First she insisted they must pose holding hands, then with their arms around each other, and finally that they should kiss.

'*Não,*' Jader said, smiling a tight smile and shaking his head.

'*Sim,*' his maid countermanded. 'You her man, she your woman. Kiss.'

Frowning, he turned to Ellen. 'There's no way out,' he muttered, beneath his breath, and he kissed her.

Compared to the previous kisses they had shared, this one ranked as commonplace; yet the touch of his lips worked their usual magic. Ellen's mouth tingled, her heart lurched, her legs went weak. She recognised that her reaction was juvenile and pathetic, yet it seemed beyond her control.

'*Muito obrigada,*' Teresa declared, beaming, and started to chatter again. She thanked the *senhor* for allowing her such a long holiday and was telling Ellen how generous and wondrously kind he was, when she suddenly realised that her friends on the other side of the road were becoming restless. '*Adeus,*' she said, in a hasty goodbye, and hurried over to rejoin them.

'You appeared to understand most of what Teresa said,' Jader remarked as, walking together now because the crowd had thinned, they set off again towards the car.

Ellen nodded. 'The longer I'm here, the more my Portuguese comes back to me.'

'Did you study it at school?'

'Yes, it was an extra choice. I took it because my teachers were keen, though also because I fancied the idea of being able to speak to Conrado in his own language.'

Jader cast her a sidelong look. 'You wanted to please him?'

Ellen shrugged. 'I guess. Of course, European Portuguese is different from the Brazilian,' she carried on, 'but he helped me with the differences, the pronunciation, and, all in all, I have a fair grounding. I just need practice.' As they went down the curving ramp of the private garage, her forehead puckered. 'Teresa called you my man and so did the woman in the dress shop,' she said, remembering.

'Marco and Nilson also thought we were sweethearts,' Jader observed.

'Anna and Leila, too.' Ellen's frown deepened. 'I wonder why everyone seems to get the wrong idea?'

Jader's brown eyes met hers. 'I wonder,' he said, and the air between them seemed to thicken.

Pressing out the code which released the side-door of the garage, he felt inside for the light switches. When they had parked earlier, the neon tubes which were the main lights had flickered intermittently, but now they did not even flicker and only a single bulb came on. It cast a small white beam in the middle of the garage, but left the remainder in darkness.

Jader stretched out a hand towards her. 'Come along,' he said.

Ellen's tension wound up a notch. For two days, he had noticeably avoided any deliberate touching and she was tempted to refuse. But he was offering help and a refusal would seem petty, she reasoned, so she took hold of the proffered hand.

Twelve spaces were marked out for vehicles in three separate rows of four and all were full. The convertible occupied the furthest space on the front row and, skirting discarded filing cabinets and broken office furniture, they made their way carefully around the gloomy perimeter.

When they reached the car, Jader let go of her hand. For a moment he stood in silence, frowning at her through the shadows, then he stepped closer. Placing one hand in the small of her back and pushing the other into the thickness of blonde hair at the back of her head, he pulled her into him. His mouth covered hers. Earlier, she recalled, his kiss had been comparatively commonplace, but this one was deep and searching. When it broke, Ellen felt wobbly.

She clutched tight at the strap of her camera bag which hung from one shoulder. 'What was that for?' she enquired, trying to appear both irritated at his impertinence and coldly unmoved, though not succeeding in either.

'It's not *for* anything. I want you, dammit!' Jader rasped, and his mouth came down on hers again.

Ellen started to push him away, but as his tongue thrust between her lips she felt a surge of sensation which stilled her hands and reduced her resistance to zero. This was not the Carnival mood she was responding to, she thought dazedly; it was Jader. Just Jader. His taste, his scent, his touch combined to make the ultimate aphrodisiac. The hands she had flattened against his shoulders slid up around his neck and Ellen pressed closer. By the time the kiss ended, they were both breathing heavily.

Reaching beyond her, Jader turned the key in his door and released the central locking. 'In the back,' he instructed as she walked around to the passenger side.

'Excuse me?'

'One of the definitions of intelligence is that you don't make the same mistake twice, but I can't help myself,' Jader muttered, and frowned. 'Get into the back seat.'

Ellen gazed at him across the bonnet of the car. Why didn't he want her to sit alongside him? she wondered, in confusion. How come she had been banished to the rear? Then, with sudden shock, she realised what he meant by 'the same mistake' and what he intended. They were to make love. In the car. In the garage. She could see the charged maleness in his eyes.

'I—I thought you were hungry?' she stammered, her mind running amok and her pulses jangling.

'I am, but I'm hungrier for you. Every time I look at you now, I see you standing in the hall, naked and proud in your black lace stockings,' he said, his voice softening and becoming husky in memory, 'and I want you.' Jader strode round to her side of the car and opened the door. 'Get inside,' he said, pulling the front seat forward.

Ellen looked at him with wide blue eyes. She wanted them to make love too. Her body cried out for his. But... But... Their relationship needed to be repaired. This was not the way things should be. Jader's mix of desire and hostility jarred.

'Somebody might see us,' she protested.

'It's dark and there's no one here.'

'But people could arrive to collect their cars.'

He was steering her into the convertible and she was letting him. Ellen's head warned that this was not the most prudent course of action—as he had said, it lacked intelligence—yet her body was yielding to her desire.

'If they do, we'll hear them,' he replied, and followed her into the magnolia leather comfort of the back seat.

Closing the door, Jader pulled her to him and they began kissing each other with a kind of desperate ferocity. As they kissed, he pushed back her skirt and slid his hands up her bare thighs. With him helping, and although she knew it was outrageous, Ellen wriggled out of her bikini briefs.

'Jader, no,' she demurred, when he started to peel off her silk jersey top.

It would be awkward enough if they were disturbed in the back of the convertible, without her being half-naked!

'I need to touch your breasts,' he said thickly.

The boat-necked top disappeared, then her bra. Now Ellen felt his hands caressing the burgeoning curves, his fingers rubbing across her distended nipples. Reaching blindly for the buttons on his shirt, she unfastened them. She needed to touch him. As her breasts brushed his chest and she felt the bitter-sweet chafing of coarse hair against her nipples, Ellen whimpered.

More of his clothes were removed in the darkness. There were more desperate kisses, more touching. Now Jader was laying her down beneath him on the leather seat and pushing into her. As she felt him, hard and hot, filling her, completing her, making her whole, Ellen whimpered again. I love you, she said silently, and, with a sob, she gave herself up to that urgent, inevitable, giddying crescendo.

Ellen stared out through the windscreen. The hurly-burly of Carnival Rio had been left behind in the distance and they were travelling along a shadowy, starlit coast. The night road was quiet. For miles they had seen only the occasional car, and, for miles, neither she nor Jader had spoken.

Ellen fingered the pearl which she wore on a gold chain round her neck. She might have no regrets about their lovemaking at the apartment, but she did rue the events of this evening, she thought bleakly. Before she had not known that Jader was destined to remain hostile, yet this time she had.

How could she have been so foolish and so biddable? she wondered, reproaching herself. Granted, the sexual impulse was a compelling force, but what had happened to her will-power and self-esteem? Her rules of conduct had not just been broken, they had been smashed to smithereens! She glanced at her chauffeur. His severe expression and silence said that he too was undergoing serious doubts about their liaison.

Ellen twisted the gold chain disconsolately around her finger. Whatever Jader felt about her, she loved him. When she had looked into his eyes at the airport and recognised what she had believed was a kindred spirit, something had touched her essential soul. Instinctively, she had known that Jader de Sa Moreira was special to her, even if she had promptly denied it, and she ought to have realised that, for her, the attraction was more than physical. Much more.

Ellen sighed. She had been attracted to him for so long. It had started with her teenage crush, yet for ten years after he had lingered in her thoughts. Jader's continuing, though unacknowledged, appeal was the reason why she had so much wanted them to be friends, she brooded, and doubtless explained why he could arouse such strong emotions within her—of fury and passion. Her heart cramped. Too much passion.

Ellen gazed out at a deserted beach which shone silver in the moonlight. If she stayed on in Rio, she would be constantly aware that Jader was somewhere around and that she just might run into him—which would condemn her to perpetual agitation. It must be better to make a clean break, she decided. So she would sell him her shares and fly out on Thursday, as he wished. That left a couple of days when she would need to ensure that there were no further sexual lapses, but she could manage two days. She could.

Ellen glanced sideways again. Besides, Jader's hard-felt misgivings would mean that, from now on, his lust would be kept under strict lock and key, she thought astringently. As for loving him—well, the logical department said that if you could fall in love you must also be able to fall out of it. And she would, Ellen resolved—given time.

'There's the restaurant,' Jader said, lifting a hand from the wheel to gesture ahead.

On the ocean side of the road stood a sprawling log-cabin-style building with a long veranda and a pitched roof. Carriage lamps gleaming around the entrance and the pink-shaded table lamps which shone in a row of gingham-curtained windows imparted a cheerful, welcoming air.

'Nice,' Ellen muttered, feeling some response was required, yet thinking that whilst he might be keen to eat she had no appetite.

Beyond the restaurant stretched a large, gravelled parking ground, and Jader swung onto it.

'I didn't expect the place to be so busy,' he said, eyeing the lengthy rows of parked cars.

They needed to go up one shadowy row, down, and up along the next before they found an empty space tucked in the middle. When Jader cut the engine, Ellen climbed out of the convertible and went around to the rear. Although a faint hum of chatter sounded from inside the restaurant, the parking ground was silent and still.

'I'd like to put my camera out of sight in the boot,' she said, when he came to join her.

'Sure.'

Jader had raised the lid and was turning to take the camera bag from her, when a figure rose out of the darkness between two adjacent cars and, in what seemed like one bound, appeared beside them. Ellen blinked. It was a swarthy, long-haired youth in a grubby grey T-shirt and sweatpants.

'*Por favor,*' he said, with a smile, and made a lunge for her camera.

Surprised, she stood frozen, but as the youth lunged

Jader also moved towards her. He grabbed the bag from her hand, swung it into the boot and slammed down the lid. Unexpectedly thwarted, the would-be thief gawked at the closed lid, looked up at Jader and across at Ellen. He seemed unsure as to what to do next, but, with a flash of a sinewy arm, he reached out, snatched the gold chain from around her neck and ran off with it between the lines of cars.

'My pearl,' Ellen said, in dismay. 'I love my pearl. It's one of my most precious possessions.'

'I'll get it back for you,' Jader declared, and with a shout at the thief to stop he sprinted after him.

She watched for a bewildered, paralysed moment and then sprang forward, following.

Glancing back at the shout and discovering he was being pursued, the youth ran faster. Jader put on an extra spurt and, behind him, Ellen increased her pace too. They were gradually drawing closer when their prey dived in between two cars and seemed to vanish into the mythical thin air.

'Where—where's he gone?' Ellen panted, arriving beside Jader. She searched the darkness. 'I can't see him.'

'Nor me.' Cutting through the row of stationary vehicles to the next aisle, Jader looked up and down. 'He must be around somewhere.'

Ellen listened. She had heard the revving of an engine and, a moment later, she saw a sleek drophead coupé, with the lines of a thinly disguised racing car, hurtling down from the top end of the aisle. The youth was driving it— she could just identify him through the windscreen—and he was heading straight for Jader.

'Watch out!' she yelled.

The path the car made was erratic and as it neared Jader it swayed towards him. With a startled oath, he flung himself clear—and slammed, half-twisted, against the high side of a four-wheel drive. Showering up gravel, the youth skidded around the end of the aisle, shot out of the parking ground and swung right onto the highway.

Ellen started towards Jader, but he was already running back. 'Are you all right?' she enquired, for he had slammed into the off-roader with some force.

He put a hand to his ribs and winced. 'It feels like I've bruised myself, but I'm still in one piece.' Taking hold of her arm, he propelled her, running, with him towards the convertible. 'We're going to catch that bastard and retrieve your pearl,' he vowed.

A couple of minutes later, they were travelling back along the coast in the direction they had come. Intent and concentrated, Jader was driving at speed. As they tore along the highway, Ellen leaned over to read the speedometer. Her eyes opened wide. The car's smooth comfort reduced the awareness of acceleration, but she had not imagined they were going *so* fast.

'We're doing almost a hundred miles an hour,' she protested.

'The road's deserted,' he replied.

'Not quite,' Ellen said as a lone truck went by on the opposite side.

They travelled on, meeting no further traffic, but with, she noticed, the speedometer creeping steadily upwards. Yet Jader's cool authority at the wheel meant that, whilst their speed amazed her, she also felt completely safe.

'Gotcha!' he declared, with a sudden hoot of triumph, and when Ellen looked ahead she saw the red tail-lights of the coupé.

'It must be stolen,' she said.

He nodded. 'It's the pick of the Italian crop,' he told her, naming a world-famous manufacturer, 'and costs megabucks. The kid didn't have enough time to break into it just now, so he must've stolen it earlier.' His eyes narrowed. 'Does that look like purple to you?'

Ellen studied the coupé. In the dark and with only the sodium glare of an occasional passing light, it was difficult to make out the true colour. But as Jader pressed his foot down harder and they drew nearer—she dreaded to think of their speed now—the shade could be defined.

'It is purple,' she said.

'In that case, I reckon it could be Roscoe Chard's swankmobile,' Jader said, and winced again.

Ellen shot him a worried look. 'Are you sure you're all right? Look, let's forget about my pearl. It isn't valuable and—'

'We're only yards away,' he protested.

'I don't care. Your state of health is far more important,' she insisted, then gave a bleat of alarm.

Realising he was on the brink of being overtaken, the youth had yanked on the wheel of the coupé and was swerving wildly across in front of them. Ellen held on tight to the edge of her seat. He did not seem to be in proper control for, the next moment, he swerved back, shot off the road and careered onto a wasteland of low pebbled sandhills.

'Thank goodness,' she said, and was exhaling a breath of relief, when Jader swung off the highway after him. 'Are you crazy?' she shouted as they bounced over the uneven ground and bounced in their seats.

He flinched. The bouncing was obviously hurting him. 'No, I'm committed,' Jader yelled back.

Following the coupé's zigzag path, he slewed around bushes and bowled over gritty sandhills. Ellen hung on for dear life. Although she had called him crazy, she knew Jader would not do anything *too* reckless, but the youth was an unknown quantity. Suppose he swung around and tried to force a collision? Or attempted to ram them? Ellen looked at Jader and frowned. He might be in dogged pursuit, but, she had suddenly realised, although he had two hands on the wheel, he was using only one to pull.

She was opening her mouth to demand that he stop, when, ahead of them, the coupé abruptly spun and dived headfirst into a hillock. There was a spraying storm of sand and stones, a scrunch of bodywork, and the engine cut out. Their pursuit had ended.

Jader brought the convertible to a halt and, as he turned off the ignition, placed a tentative hand on his shoulder.

'Are you still in one piece?' Ellen asked anxiously.

'Or two,' he replied, with a dismissive smile, and climbed awkwardly out to confront the thief.

The driver's door was buckled and the youth needed to thump at it several times before he could open it. As he stood upright, Ellen eyed him warily. He looked shaken but uninjured, so would he sprint off again?

'*Não!*' Jader rapped, when the youth went to put his hand into his trouser pocket.

Goose-pimples shivered her skin. Oh, heavens! Ellen thought, in alarm. He has a gun. Having avoided a car crash, are we going to be shot? But, after patting his sweatpants to demonstrate that he was unarmed, the thief produced the pearl and gold chain, and handed it to her.

'Um—*obrigada*,' she faltered.

'Sorry for taking it,' he said, in Portuguese, and shone her a disarming smile. 'I just needed to take something. But that was fun, like being in a car chase in a movie.'

'He's saying he enjoyed the chase,' Jader started to translate.

'So I gathered, but I was petrified!' Ellen protested.

'You could've killed yourself and us,' Jader told him.

'*Não.*'

'*Sim,*' he insisted. 'If you'd turned the coupé over—and you were close at times—it could've caught fire and you might've been trapped inside and burned to death.'

A laid-back and surprisingly charming character, the boy considered this for a moment, then shrugged. Looking beyond them to the convertible, he began to sing its praises. The danger, and his crimes, seemed inconsequential and it was the car's performance which grabbed his interest.

'He's impressed with our speed and how easily we caught up with him,' Jader said, in a dry-voiced translation. 'He says he's seen Moreiras around, but never bothered to steal one. However—' he laughed and immediately winced '—he reckons that next time he wants wheels he'll look out for one. I'm honoured,' he said, with a sardonic bow of his head, and explained that he was Senhor de Sa Moreira and it was his company which manufactured the cars.

Now doubly impressed, the youth launched into questions about horsepower, acceleration and top speeds. Jader answered him, his enthusiasm for the convertible taking precedence over his physical discomfort.

'Is this Roscoe Chard's car?' Ellen enquired, when the information-gathering session came to an end.

The boy nodded. 'I took it from outside a hotel where the guy was partying.'

'He's not going to be too pleased when he sees what you've done to it,' Jader remarked, eyeing the buckled door and stoved-in bonnet.

The culprit shrugged. 'He can afford another.'

'I'm a journalist,' Ellen told him, 'and I'd like to write an article about why you decided to steal the coupé and how you steal others. Would you be willing to tell me?'

'For sure,' he agreed, grinning. 'You want to take a picture of me beside the coupé?' he suggested.

'OK.'

Ellen retrieved her camera and took several flash-bulb shots of him posing proudly. 'What's your name?' she asked, opening the notepad which she always carried.

'Pepe.'

Relishing the attention, Pepe talked about his method, went on to explain how he loved joyriding and had begun to shamelessly boast of how he specialised in stealing quality fast cars, when there was the sound of a siren. The three of them turned, to see a police car with lights flashing bouncing over the sand.

'That was quick,' Pepe said, when two police officers clambered out of the car and came towards them. He had shown no desire to make a run for it; he seemed to be having too good a time talking about his exploits.

'Someone saw you being chased and rang to report it on their mobile phone,' the younger of the officers replied.

The older man, who was thick-set with greying hair, looked at Pepe and rolled his eyes. He uttered a few complaining words of recognition, and spoke to Jader. 'What's been happening, *senhor*?' he enquired.

Jader explained, but as soon as he had finished Pepe started to speak, telling the policemen of his admiration for the convertible and suggesting, in all seriousness, that the Rio police department should consider purchasing Moreiras for their fleet in future.

'Thanks for the plug,' Jader said wryly, and grimaced.

Ellen had been making continuous notes, but she stopped to frown at him. His face was pale and drawn, and he had a hand cupped around his shoulder as if he needed to protect it. She stepped closer.

'I think you've broken something,' she said.

Jader gave a strained smile. 'Could be.'

'You're hurt, *senhor*,' the older policeman declared. 'I'll call an ambulance.'

Ellen put her hand on Jader's good arm. 'Come and sit down,' she said, and led him back to the convertible.

'What about the car?' he said as she hovered anxiously over him. 'Could you drive it back to the apartment? You're worried about the traffic?' he asked, when she frowned.

'No, it's you I'm worried about,' Ellen told him, 'and I'd prefer to come to the hospital with you.'

'Thanks,' he said, and managed another strained smile. 'I'd prefer it too.'

'We can deliver your car to your home, *senhor*,' the older police officer called, overhearing them.

'It'd be our pleasure,' declared the younger one, and as they waited for the ambulance the two policemen and Pepe walked admiringly around the Moreira and discussed its appeal.

Although the ambulance took some time to arrive, when they arrived at the hospital Jader was quickly examined.

'A small bone in his shoulder has been broken and the X-ray revealed two cracked ribs,' a sister in starched whites informed Ellen, in brisk Portuguese. 'There's always a risk of delayed shock, so we shall keep the patient in overnight, but you may collect him at noon tomorrow.'

'Don't forget,' said Jader, who was lying on a stretcher as he waited for his injuries to be strapped up.

Ellen lifted her brows. 'As if.'

'I'm sorry you didn't get to watch the rest of the Carnival parade,' he said.

'I'm sorry you smashed yourself up,' she told him ruefully.

'I'll mend.

'Why are you so attached to your pearl?' Jader suddenly enquired, when they had said goodbye and a porter was on the point of wheeling him away. 'Did someone you care for give it to you?'

Ellen nodded. 'It was a gift from Conrado.'

CHAPTER SEVEN

ROSCOE CHARD turned up the collar of his monogrammed, midnight-blue designer shirt, showed his right profile—his better profile—to the camera, and reached out to shake Jader's left hand, the one which was not in a sling.

'Ready,' he told Ellen, and lifted his chin.

When the police had advised him that Senhor de Sa Moreira had been instrumental in the recovery of his car, and when he had read the subsequent newspaper report, he had not realised the chief executive of the Moreira empire was so much younger than him nor so good-looking. The actor tilted his chin a little higher. He prayed his jaw-line did not look crepey in comparison.

Recognising the strategy, Ellen bit down on a grin. Tall, tanned and with his blond hair swept back from his brow, in the flesh Roscoe Chard looked surprisingly weathered and lined for a man who claimed to be in his early forties. Did they film his close-ups through gauze? she wondered as she took photographs on the terrace. Might the rather orangey tan come out of a bottle?

'You're producing one helluva of an automobile,' the actor declared, when Ellen had completed the shots she required and the three of them returned to the living room. 'Magnificent styling, engine as smooth as butter and great power.'

'We believe in it,' Jader replied.

They had recently returned from a run in the convertible

with Roscoe Chard at the wheel and since hearing the first purr of the engine he had been paying glowing tributes and scattering superlatives.

'I've spotted a few Moreiras when I've been in town and always admired their handsome looks,' he went on and paused to smooth down a sideburn, as if signifying a parallel with his own glamorous Hollywood appearance. 'But it was only when I learned how swiftly you'd caught up with my machine and detained the thief that their true class hit home. And after driving the convertible—and a man in my position drives the most prestigious of high-performance cars,' he stated, 'I'm very, very excited by it.'

'Thank you,' Jader said, and arched a brow at Ellen.

She grinned back. So far, things were going to plan.

'May I top up your champagne?' she asked their visitor.

Having first had an aide telephone to announce that his master wished to visit to impart his sincere thanks for the retrieval of his car *in person*, Roscoe Chard had arrived early this afternoon armed with an enormous bouquet of flowers and two magnums of champagne. His emphatic insistence on their excellent vintage had indicated a desire for a cork to be popped immediately and he had already downed his second glass. It did not matter that Jader was on painkillers, could not drink alcohol and so had soda, nor that Ellen had only taken a few obliging sips—their benefactor was consuming his gift with gusto.

'That'd be great, honey,' he declared, and watched as Ellen walked over to the bureau to pour a refill.

With her blonde hair and that lissom figure in mauve T-shirt and jeans, the girl *was* a honey, he thought. He tugged at the waistband of his close-fitting moleskin trousers. Should he say he could arrange a film test? Maybe not; she had a boyfriend and—the crucial factor—gave no sign of being in awe of him and his fame. He preferred females who were in awe.

'You've explained you're in journalism,' he continued, accepting the brimming glass, 'so did you write the report on the theft which I read in the paper?'

Ellen sat down again. She and Jader were in the arm-chairs—Jader with a cushion at his back to provide support—while Roscoe Chard was sprawled half across the sofa. He reminded her of an emperor, granting an audience to minions.

'Almost, but not quite,' she replied. 'I took my account into the office and asked if they'd be interested in printing it.'

'Which they were,' the actor declared, before she could get any further. 'The media *devours* news about anyone with a name.' He gulped down another mouthful of champagne. 'And the bigger the name, the more ecstatic they are.'

Ellen gave a silent groan. Although she had covered current news, political crises and such, her work had brought her into occasional contact with members of the entertainment world, but she had never met anyone as famous as Roscoe Chard. Nor had she ever met anyone who was such a chronic believer in his own hype!

'However, because I wasn't a hundred per cent certain of my Portuguese I spoke with an English-speaking reporter,' she continued, 'a man who used to work for the *Los Angeles Times*. He altered a few words, though it's an accurate account.'

'Entirely,' Jader confirmed.

'I have a house in L.A. In Beverly Hills—a most exclusive neighbourhood,' the actor said. 'I have four homes—there, here, an apartment in London and a villa on a private island in the Caribbean.'

'Fascinating,' Ellen murmured, scribbling the information on her notepad for this was clearly what he expected. 'I suggested to the reporter that he might care to wire the story on to Los Angeles and that's what he's done.'

Roscoe Chard shone his mega-white, trademark smile. He thrived on publicity, of whatever kind. A day when he failed to feature in the media in some way was a day consigned to purgatory.

'Sensible girl. My fans always appreciate news of me,' he announced, as if Ellen had performed some noble, needy, life-saving service.

'And I've spoken to an associate in London who writes a gossip column,' she told him. 'He says he'll drop in a mention.'

The stagey white smile shone again. 'I have many devoted followers in England.'

'I also asked the Rio editor if he'd be interested in a longer article explaining how Pepe, the thief, came to steal your car, our pursuit and your response,' Ellen went on. 'He is.'

Although they had explained how Jader had followed the coupé with the aim of retrieving her pearl, Roscoe Chard had blithely ignored this fact and centred the incident entirely on himself. He might not have been there or known anything about it, yet, as at the cinema, he was the star. As a celluloid leading man, for him to settle for a bit part in real life was apparently inconceivable.

'You'd illustrate it with the handshake shot and a couple of those of me beside the convertible which you took when we were out?' he enquired.

'Essential,' Jader pronounced, straight-faced, and when the actor replied with a solemn nod of agreement Ellen almost giggled.

'I have contacts which mean I could get the article syndicated worldwide,' she said, and added unnecessarily, 'If you're willing?'

'It's a swell idea,' Roscoe Chard vowed, and fell silent, recalling the earlier shots. Handsome man with luxury fast car—it had a powerfully sexual resonance. Should he demand that only those photographs which featured him alone be used? he wondered. His gaze went to the bureau and the gifts which he had brought. No, it could seem ungracious. 'I'm grateful to you for seizing the joyrider,' he told Jader. 'If you hadn't stopped him when you did, he could've decided to do handbrake skids, or whatever it is the kids do these days, and written off my machine in total.' He heaved a much put-upon sigh. 'As it is, the repair shop reckons it'll take a month to fix.'

'We thought it could take a while,' Jader said, 'and we'd like to offer you the free use of a Moreira in the meantime.' He looked at Ellen. 'I say "we" because Ellen is a fellow director.'

'That's real generous. As you'll realise, I'm a busy man with many demands on my time and anything which helps make life a little easier is most welcome,' Roscoe Chard declared, in a gooey acceptance speech.

'We could also spray a convertible purple for you,' Ellen said, and turned to check with Jader who nodded. 'If you wish.'

'Thanks, but that was a girlfriend's idea and—' the actor grimaced '—I got kinda bored with her and kinda bored with purple. Scarlet has more style.'

'I'll arrange to have a scarlet convertible delivered to you tomorrow morning,' Jader told him. 'Around eleven?'

'Perfect.'

'And if, when your own car's repaired, you should become bored with it and fancy buying a Moreira,' he continued, 'we'd be willing to give you a special deal.'

Roscoe Chard's grey eyes gleamed. He might make millions of dollars per movie and live in luxury, but he appreciated a bargain. He was not a 'tight wad', as the girl responsible for the purple had accused before walking out on him; he simply knew the value of money.

'I'll most certainly consider it,' he enthused.

'There's something else which perhaps you could consider,' Jader said thoughtfully. 'The joyrider—Pepe. He's hooked on cars and a pretty fair driver, and I was wondering whether—once the courts have done their duty— you might be able to arrange for him to watch a car chase being organised for a movie? It'd help make the kid aware of the dangers involved, the safety consciousness employed and, hopefully, teach him a sense of responsibility.'

The actor toyed with the golden nugget which dangled around his neck. For some strange reason, his public image did not come over too well and his agent had suggested he should make a determined effort to improve it. Like today's thank-you, showing an interest in the thief would be another gesture which could be circulated to demonstrate his human touch and his kindness—yet it was a kindness which would cost cash.

'Gee...' he began, wondering how he could caringly decline.

'I'd pay for Pepe's flight to the States and his living expenses for a couple of months,' Jader said.

Roscoe Chard's mental grip on his wallet eased. 'I shall have a word with a pal who's a stunt organiser and fix for the kid to meet him. And suggest that maybe he could find him a job connected with stunts.'

Jader grinned. 'I'm sure Pepe would be grateful.'

'Always ready to help those less fortunate,' the actor declared bluffly. Draining the last drop of champagne, he rose to his feet. 'Get well soon,' he told him, and turned his dazzling white smile onto Ellen. 'Real nice to meet you. You will remember to put the name of my next movie in your article?' he said as she walked with him out to the lift. He passed a hand over his hair. 'Personally, I don't envision it'll bring me yet another nomination for an Oscar, but informed opinion appears to believe that it will.'

'I'll mention the film,' she assured him.

'Thanks, honey.' Roscoe Chard wondered again whether to suggest a film test, but decided against it. 'Goodbye.'

'Let's hear it for Mr Wonderful,' Jader said drolly, when she returned to the living room.

Ellen laughed. 'You shouldn't mock the afflicted.'

'You're referring to the outsize ego, the face lift and the corset?'

'Plus the fact that he's forty-two going on fifty. Still, he did seem very impressed with the convertible and it wouldn't surprise me if he bought one.'

'Here's hoping, because he'd make it known and give us street cred.' Reaching out with care, for his chest was strapped and tightly bandaged, Jader put down his glass of soda. 'It has occurred to you that, speed for speed, power for power, the convertible and Chard's coupé are similar?' he said. 'And that the reason I caught up was because Pepe was unused to his vehicle whereas I know the Moreira inside out?'

'It has,' Ellen replied, 'and I don't doubt other people will realise it too. But all that matters is my being able to write an article which isn't an advertisement and which could generate sales.'

'Especially when everyone sees the photographs of Roscoe Chard,' Jader said sardonically.

'It was kind of him to come to say thank you,' she protested.

'A public relations exercise,' he dismissed.

'Cynic.'

Jader grinned, unrepentant. 'I liked your purple suggestion,' he said.

'I liked your idea of him arranging for Pepe to be present at the filming of a car chase,' Ellen responded. 'And it'd be good if he could get him a job.'

'If he doesn't, I'll fix the kid up with something and try to break his cycle of crime.'

She smiled. 'So everything's worked out even better than we hoped.'

'Thanks to your brainwave of writing about the chase,' Jader said.

'And thanks to your idea of loaning Roscoe Chard a car.'

He grinned. 'We make a good double act.'

Ellen took a sip of champagne. Since the accident two days ago, Jader's formality and aloofness had gone. Though, to be realistic, it would have been difficult for him to remain aloof with her acting as his helpmate and general factotum. She had made his meals, cut up his food, helped Jader to dress—leaving him to struggle with underpants and trousers—and even braved the traffic and driven to the local supermarket to buy fresh groceries. And together they had worked out their scheme for provoking the actor's interest in the Moreira.

They did make a good double act, Ellen brooded, yet the operative word was 'act'. Jader was pretending he had forgotten his deep-down hostility, while she was performing the role of someone whose emotions were bland, unconcerned and in control. What a sham! She felt so wound up and so in love with him that, at times, it was all she could do not to fling herself tempestuously at his feet and declare that love.

'You told Roscoe Chard I was a fellow director,' Ellen

said. 'Thanks, but I want to sell you my shares. So as soon as you can arrange witnesses—'

'Some time,' Jader muttered distractedly. 'I must ring the sales manager and get him to have a car delivered to Chard tomorrow,' he said, 'and speaking of double acts—' He ran a hand over the faint blue-black shadow on his jaw. 'If I apply the foam, would you wield the razor?'

'Yes, master,' Ellen agreed pertly, and added, 'We can't let the invalid look scruffy for his visitors.'

As soon as her report had appeared in the newspaper that morning, the telephone had begun to ring. Many of his friends—including Anna, Leila and husbands, and even some from São Paulo—and business colleagues and employees had called, wanting to know the details and anxious for an update on Jader's injuries. And at intervals ever since people had been arriving at the door, with flowers, chocolates, and good wishes.

Some, like Teresa, the maid, and the gardener from the apartments, could ill afford their gifts, and their concern had made her realise how much Jader was liked and how caring he must be of others. Ellen ached. If only he could give her a little of that caring.

'Shall I dial the sales manager for you?' she asked, indicating the phone on the bureau.

Jader nodded. 'Please.'

When he had been connected to the number, Ellen went through to his bathroom. Because his right hand was out of use, Jader also required assistance with shaving. She had shaved him twice before and now she took shaving cream and a safety razor from the cabinet. The water was run until it came hot and she prepared a towel.

'All fixed,' Jader informed her, coming in a few minutes later. 'I also need to ring the general manager in São Paulo and let him know I'll be up here and out of action for a while. But I'll do it afterwards.' Standing in front of her, he grinned. 'Buttons, please.'

As it did whenever she was required to help him with his clothes, to touch him, Ellen's heart started to race. Telling herself to be cool and calm, and present an unflustered exterior, she undid the buttons and helped him off with his shirt.

'You intend to stay on in Rio, rather than go home?' she asked, trying not to notice the healthy golden sheen of his shoulders and the way his hair lay at the nape of his neck.

His hair covered his head in thick dark waves of the running-your-fingers-through variety and ended at his collar in a fringe of tiny curls.

'I do.' Jader adjusted the triangular sling which supported his arm. 'I shall need help after tomorrow,' he said.

Tomorrow was Thursday—the day she had told him she would be quitting his apartment and the day she intended to leave Rio. Frowning, Ellen hung up his shirt on a hook. She had been so busy getting her article published and looking after him, she had given no thought to her departure and the reminder came as a shock. Disappointment formed a cold nub inside her. She did not feel ready to leave Brazil, though it was, she told herself, merely a matter of becoming mentally attuned to the idea.

'I'm sure Teresa would be willing to act as nursemaid,' Ellen said. 'Or one of your friends. Or you could hire in help.'

'I'd prefer you to stay,' Jader said, looking at her with steady brown eyes. 'Would you?'

'Yes,' she replied, and heard herself answer too quickly. 'I—well, you hurt yourself trying to help me by getting back the pearl, so it's only right I should help you by remaining here and looking after you,' Ellen jabbered, in an attempt to justify her immediate acquiescence both to him and to herself. Making a grab at the bathroom stool, she placed it beside the basin. 'Sit down, please.'

She could have stayed on in Rio, but why had she agreed to remain with him in his apartment? Ellen wondered as she unscrewed the cap on the shaving cream and Jader started to lather his cheeks. It made no sense when helping him, simply being close to him disturbed her. Yet, contrarily, she *wanted* to help. She had never imagined herself as an amateur nurse before, but she enjoyed caring for him.

Ellen placed the towel around his shoulders. By remaining, she might be putting her emotions through the wringer, but she was not entering any dangerous sexual waters. Jader's ribs, which he complained were painful, would be strapped up for three weeks and she was going home in three weeks. Ergo, there was no chance of passion taking control, no risk of—her heart thumped—lovemaking.

'I am yours to do with as you wish,' Jader declared, grinning at her like a foam-bearded Santa Claus.

Ellen shone him a wafer-thin smile, stood beside him, and carefully and methodically began to draw the razor down his face.

'I'll make sure that looking after me doesn't disrupt the photography you plan to do around Rio,' he said, when she broke off to rinse the blade.

'Thanks,' she said, and frowned, suddenly wondering why he should want her to stay.

Perhaps Jader thought that as he had paid to bring her out to Rio she might as well earn her keep? Or maybe— she noticed his gaze glancing over her breasts—he had decided that having a watchable blonde around would help relieve the boredom of his convalescence?

'Careful!' Jader protested as she sliced briskly down over his top lip. 'I'd prefer to keep my nose.'

'So sorry,' she said.

The remainder of his whiskers were removed, streaks of foam washed away, his face dried. He checked his jaw. 'Perfect. Now you pat on aftershave,' he told her.

Ellen's nerves tingled. 'You didn't have aftershave last time,' she protested.

Jader smiled benignly. 'I forgot.'

He knew that touching him disturbed her, she thought furiously as she took the bottle from the cabinet, and he was doing this on purpose.

'Don't even think about it,' Jader said, his eyes meeting hers in the mirror as she sprinkled her palms with the spicily fragrant liquid.

'About what?'

'Slapping instead of patting. I may have one arm out of action, but the other is strong and active.' He allowed a few moments to go by, let her bend over him and dab the aftershave around his jaw. 'As are other parts of my body. Yes, being close to you excites me,' Jader went on as two hectic spots of colour began to burn on her cheeks. 'And although I'm currently unable to bed you in the conventional way there are still certain sexual acts which we could indulge in.' He hoisted a brow. 'All it takes is a little imagination.'

Her face scarlet and with her heart pounding erratically, Ellen stood back. Her imagination was working overtime. 'I don't...I mean...no,' she babbled.

The doorbell rang.

Jader's mouth tweaked. 'Saved by the bell,' he murmured. 'Perhaps it's Mr Wonderful, coming back to tell us he's decided to buy a convertible.'

'Say a prayer,' Ellen told him, and hurried thankfully off to answer it.

But when she opened the door the caller was a plump, snub-nosed brunette. She wore a brown jacket and pleated skirt, and carried a large shopping bag. She could only be in her early thirties, yet had a matronly, middle-aged air. Beside her stood a solemn brown-eyed boy, while two little girls in pretty flowered dresses giggled in the background. Looking closer at the boy, Ellen recognised a schoolboy Jader.

'You must be Yolanda,' she said, smiling at the woman and speaking in Portuguese.

'I am,' the caller confirmed, in the same language. She subjected her to a piercing look. 'You are Ellen Blanchard,' she declared, and, with a waft of a hand which summoned her children forward, she strode past her and into the hall.

'*Ola,*' Jader said, coming out from the bathroom where, somehow, he had managed to put on his shirt and fasten it.

His stepmother acknowledged him with a curt bob of her permed brown head and the boy grinned, but the little girls squealed out his name and rushed forward to greet him.

'Careful,' he warned, fending off the most exuberant of their hugs but returning their kisses. 'I've hurt my shoulder and cracked some ribs, so I'm sore.' He reached out towards the boy who, seeming to feel himself too old for such childish behaviour, hovered a yard or so away. 'How's Master Luiz?' he enquired, putting his arm around him.

Pleased to be included, the boy smiled. 'Fine. We read about you in the paper,' he told him.

'I read it first,' the younger of the little girls boasted. 'I'm good at reading.'

'No, it was me,' Luiz protested.

As a small argument broke out, with Jader acting as a pacifying referee, Ellen watched the scene. She had known he was fond of his small half-brother and half-sisters, but she had not realised how easy he would be with them, nor how easy they would be with him. She felt a twinge. He was like a second father and, when the time came, would be a good father to his own children.

'We brought you these,' one of the little girls said, darting back to her mother to dip into the shopping bag.

She produced a lollipop, while her sister gave him a bag of sweets and her brother handed over a chocolate egg.

'They bought them with their pocket money,' Yolanda told him proudly.

'I shall enjoy every bite,' Jader declared, and there were more hugs and kisses all round.

'Would you care for coffee?' Ellen asked Yolanda. The conversation had been in Portuguese and she used the same language. 'Would the children like a cold drink?'

The brunette nodded. 'Thank you. Cola?' she said to her offspring, and all three nodded.

'If you go into the living room, I'll bring the drinks through,' Ellen said.

Jader smiled. 'Thanks.'

She made the coffee and set out a tray. Ellen had just filled a plate with chocolate biscuits when Yolanda walked into the kitchen.

'Ever since I discovered that my husband left you shares in his car company, I've been wondering what you look like,' she said, speaking in sharp, cool and surprisingly good English.

Ellen gave a cautious smile. The look she had received

at the front door had been too beady-eyed for comfort and the fact that the visitor had come to confront her on her own made her uneasy. Was she about to be told she had no right to the shares? Might she be accused of unfair practice?

'I never expected a bequest,' she said, but Yolanda had other things on her mind.

'You must've been very young when you knew Conrado,' she declared.

'Fifteen, sixteen,' Ellen replied.

'I was twenty-two when I met him.' There was a significant pause. 'When *our* romance began.'

Ellen stared. She had heard the emphasis and recognised the implication. 'I didn't have a romance with Conrado,' she said.

Yolanda's brows knitted. 'You were not his mistress?'

'Good grief, no!'

There was another pause. 'Then it must've been your mother. It was,' the brunette declared, with abrupt conviction. 'It was Vivienne whom he had loved so much and never stopped loving. I am correct, yes?'

Ellen frowned. Yolanda did not seem concerned that her husband should have continued to care for another woman throughout their marriage, only that she had mistaken the identity of that woman.

'You are,' she agreed.

'I'd always believed it was Vivienne, but when Conrado left the shares to you—' She gave a dismissive shrug.

'Natalya's decided she wants orange juice instead of cola,' Jader said, and Ellen spun round to find him standing in the doorway with the smaller of the little girls clinging onto his hand.

She smiled at the child. 'Orange juice coming up,' she told her, reverting to Portuguese.

As Yolanda returned to the living room—her mission complete—Ellen loaded the try and carried it through. Helping herself to a biscuit, Jader's stepmother ignored his injuries and how they had occurred, and started to talk about her daughter's cough, which the doctor, foolish man, had dismissed as nothing serious. This led into a virtual spot-by-spot account of how her offspring had each had measles last year, followed by a round-up of their activities in Campos de Jordão, and next came a report on her parents' holiday in the States.

'We speak every day,' she explained, wiping crumbs from her mouth.

Yolanda went on to explain, at length, how the children had insisted on calling in to see Jader on the way home from their holiday, but that now there were cases to be unpacked, a meal to be eaten, baths to be had, and—they must go.

In the midst of fussily gathering together her brood, she gave Ellen a vague nod of farewell.

'Nice to meet you,' Yolanda said, her dismissive air making it plain that she had no further interest either in her or in the shares which she had inherited.

When goodbyes had been said and Jader had trooped the family off to the lift, Ellen started collecting up glasses and plates. Yolanda *was* very different from her mother, she thought, with a frown. The woman was cold of manner, mind-numbingly domestic and wrapped up in herself. But the most striking—and tragic—difference was that she had never appreciated Conrado. She had had a gem of a husband, yet she had not noticed.

'I've been too hard on you,' Jadder said seriously as he came up the steps into the living room.

Ellen looked at him. 'Yes?' she said, wondering what was going to come next.

'I was too hard ten years ago, too quick to jump to conclusions and condemn, and since you arrived in Rio I've been too hard on you again. I apologise.' He sat down on the arm of an armchair. 'I guess that after blaming you for Conrado's distress and being angry for so long it had become a habit. But now that I've got to know you I realise you'd never trample over people's feelings and deliberately hurt them.

'I also realise that nobody's perfect,' he continued, with a frown, 'least of all me, and I accept that there are situations where you genuinely can't help yourself. So—' Jader gave a crooked smile of appeal '—do you think you could manage to forgive me? Do you think we could cancel out the past and start again?'

'I do, and I'm sure we can,' Ellen said, and sank down on the sofa.

At last, his hostility was over. She wanted to laugh. She wanted to cry. She wanted to shout her relief from the rooftops.

'Yolanda thought you must've been my father's mistress,' Jader went on slowly.

She looked across at him. 'You heard.'

'I couldn't help it, but you were speaking English and, thankfully, Natalya didn't understand.' He hesitated. 'You weren't his mistress, but you loved Conrado.'

'Very much,' Ellen agreed.

'And it was your love which made his marriage to Vivienne impossible.'

'Excuse me?'

'Vivienne had realised the depth of your feelings, realised that if she married him it would be hell for you and could only wreck your relationship with her,' Jader said, as if he was thinking his way through. 'And because she felt guilty about leaving you as a child—'

'I loved Conrado, but I loved him as a father!' Ellen protested. 'He replaced the one I'd never known.'

'He did?' Jader said, in confusion.

'Yes! When I went away for weekends with him and my mother, I used to hope that everyone would think he was my dad. And if people did I never corrected them—I was just so *pleased*. When Conrado went out of my life, he left a huge gap and I cried myself to sleep for weeks. And—' tears were suddenly stinging at the back of her eyes and she blinked them away '—when you wrote to tell me he'd died I wept again.'

Jader came to sit beside her. 'He loved you too,' he said, placing a soothing hand on her arm.

'Yes.' Ellen frowned. 'And now that another of your theories has bitten the dust I suppose you're going to demand that I tell you the real reason why I ended their affair,' she said stiffly.

Jader shook his head. 'Obviously I'd like you to be honest with me, Ellie,' he said, 'but if you prefer to remain silent that's up to you. And, from now on, I intend to keep an open mind and not pass any more judgements.'

Ellen looked at him. She did not know whether it was due to his lack of insistence, or because he had called her Ellie, or perhaps because she loved him—but, all of a sudden, she needed to tell him the truth.

'I ended their affair, with my mother's full agreement, because—' she gulped in a breath '—during the years she lived in Paris she was a call-girl.'

Jader stared at her. 'What?'

'Vivienne used to be a hooker,' Ellen told him. 'A prostitute. A whore!'

CHAPTER EIGHT

THE hand which Jader had placed on her arm tightened. 'For heaven's sake!' he said.

Ellen managed a wan smile. 'You would never've guessed?'

'Not in a million years.'

'Neither did Conrado and nor has anyone else, though my mother's clever at inventing backgrounds and playing parts.'

'But Vivienne is so elegant, so…cultured,' he said, in wondering bemusement.

'And she worked for an extremely select establishment. It wasn't touting for trade on street corners, it was being whisked to an assignation in a chauffeur-driven limousine. But you agree their relationship had to be sacrificed?' Ellen demanded. 'You understand that I *had* to tell Conrado?'

'God Almighty, yes!' Jader exclaimed.

Relief drained out of her, leaving her weak. Although she had insisted that her reasons were valid, there had been times in the past, and more recently on discovering how Conrado had suffered from the break-up, when Ellen had found herself wondering if she had been right to intervene. Should fate have been allowed to take its own course? Might she have created more trouble, rather than less? If she had stood on the sidelines, wouldn't everything have worked out fine? Her thoughts had swung agonisingly to and fro, and now Jader's reassurance was like balm to her soul.

'Thank you,' she said.

His dark brows lowered. 'Why didn't Vivienne tell him herself?' he enquired.

'She said she couldn't, that it was too painful, so—' Ellen shrugged.

'She left her sixteen-year-old daughter, to explode the bomb all on her own and deal with the fallout?' he protested.

'There wasn't much fallout.' She shot him a sideways glance. 'Not from Conrado.'

'But I came down on you like the wrath of God,' Jader said, his face gaunt, all strained angles. 'I've been such a bastard.'

'You had your reasons.'

'The wrong damn reasons!' he rasped, chastising himself.

Ellen gave a rueful smile. 'You couldn't know. Although Conrado felt aggrieved that my mother should've deceived him, he was too shocked to be angry,' she continued. 'He listened to what I had to say, asked a few questions, and stumbled out.'

'He was still shocked when he stumbled into our hotel room a quarter of an hour later,' Jader told her. 'He looked dreadful, so ill that, at first, I wondered if he might be having a heart attack. I asked him what the matter was and, although he was damn near incoherent, managed to work out that he'd come from your apartment where he'd met with you and now his romance with Vivienne was over.

'It didn't make sense. They'd spent the previous evening very happily together, so why, all of a sudden and with no advance warning, was she giving him the push? And what role did you play in it? I did my best to find out, but he wouldn't give me a straight answer. Or much of any kind of an answer. Conrado just kept shaking his head and muttering disjointed phrases about him and Vivienne having "no future", and "irreconcilable differences", and how "poor Ellie" hadn't wanted to ruin things, but had felt compelled.'

'Which made you think I must be directly involved?'

He nodded. 'In some way, yes. And that's why I stampeded round to see you. I left the hotel intending to demand a complete recital of what you'd said, but on the way over I began to think of my father's grief and that wound me up, and by the time I arrived—' Jader heaved a sigh '—I was full of righteous indignation and hopping mad.'

'I thought you were going to tear me limb from limb,' Ellen said wryly.

'It was a near thing, believe me.'

'Conrado didn't say anything unfavourable about my mother?' she enquired.

'Not a word. In fact, after that he clammed up and said nothing about her, period. And whenever I tried to talk about her, which I did initially, in the hope of discovering what had gone so dreadfully wrong, he refused to respond. But there was no hint of criticism of Vivienne, ever.'

'Because he still loved her,' Ellen said sadly.

'Yes.' Jader was silent and brooding for a moment, then he frowned. 'You said you had Vivienne's "agreement" that you should reveal her...history, so does that mean she'd been against my father knowing?'

'She was reluctant. She seemed to think—to hope—she could ignore it.'

'She would've kept quiet and gone ahead and become his wife?' he protested.

Ellen sighed. 'It's possible. She did love him, in her way, and she wanted to settle down. I knew Conrado would be shocked and terribly hurt by what I revealed, but I couldn't let her marry him under false pretences.'

'Out of the question,' Jader agreed.

'My mother may have had the idea that if she waited until after they were married and then broke the news he'd accept it,' Ellen went on. 'But it would've been criminal to condemn Conrado to the constant worry of her previous activities perhaps being discovered and spending the rest of his life on the brink of scandal. And there is always a chance of discovery,' she said, shuddering as a memory rose up in her mind to haunt her. 'There's always a risk that some man somewhere at some time will recognise Vivienne as a woman he once bought.'

Jader's brown eyes were dark and bleak. 'Conrado would never have accepted her history,' he said. 'He'd have been appalled to think that other men had paid to have sex with his wife. And deeply shamed. No matter how much he loved Vivienne, it would've soured their marriage and ended it. As, indeed, him knowing the truth brought an end to their affair.'

Ellen nodded. 'When I told him, Conrado declared straight away that he couldn't see my mother again. He never, for one second, considered that their romance might continue, let alone that marriage remained an option.'

'Is the man who married Vivienne aware of her past?' Jader asked curiously.

'Yes, Bernard was one of her clients. Like I told you, he's French and maybe that means he has a broader outlook,' Ellen said wryly, when his brows lifted. 'Though several of the girls from the same establishment have married men who know about their pasts. And they've married well—one to a New York investment banker, one to a

Spanish duke, while another is the wife of the heir to a shipping fortune.' She attempted a smile. 'Different people have differ-ent attitudes.'

'But you hate the idea of a woman selling herself for sex,' Jader said.

'I loathe it,' Ellen declared, swallowing to ease the stiffness which had tightened her throat. She was trying to be detached and unemotional, though it was difficult when her mother's past touched so dramatically on her own life and was so distasteful. 'And whilst Vivienne's explained why she did it I still find it impossible to understand how she *could*.'

'And me,' Jader muttered. 'How long have you known she was a hooker?' he enquired. 'When did she tell you?'

'She didn't. I discovered by chance, when I was fourteen, after she'd given up "the game",' Ellen said brittly, 'and returned to live in England.' She needed to swallow again. 'I was told by a girl at school who announced the news with great relish.'

'Oh, Ellie,' he said, and put his arm around her. For a long moment, he held her close against his bandaged chest as if needing to protect her from the cruelties of the world, then he looked soberly down. 'Do you want to tell me about it?'

Ellen hesitated. This far, revealing the truth had been painful and, if she continued, it seemed destined to become more so. But Jader was sympathetic. An inner voice warned that his sympathy could be transitory, yet it was compelling.

'Please,' she said. 'I've only ever told one person—a boyfriend—and I gave him just the bare outline, but—' she shone a wavery smile '—talking is reckoned to be therapeutic.'

He drew her back against the cushions of the sofa,

though his arm remained around her. 'So talk,' he encouraged.

Ellen was quiet for a minute or two, arranging her thoughts. 'My mother was always keen that I should go to a good school, which in her terms meant a private school,' she began. 'When she was in France, I attended one which was close to my grandparents' home in Kent, but after her return I switched to a far swankier girls' academy in London—'

'You said you lived with your father's folks,' Jader interrupted. 'What about your mother's parents?'

'They separated when she was twenty. Her father went off to work abroad and they lost touch, and a year or two later her mother died. So I've never seen either of them. But they seem to have been a feckless couple, who didn't care too much about each other or about Vivienne. Whereas my gran and grandad are a devoted couple and big on family.'

'You were happy living with them?' he enquired.

Ellen smiled. 'Very, and we still keep in close touch. Several of the girls at the London school came from upper-crust families,' she said, resuming her account, 'and one of them, Priscilla, had an elder brother called Torquil. Priscilla was a snooty individual at the best of times, but one morning she produced a picture of her brother with my mother, who, she announced in her ringing, carrying, cut-glass voice, was a common tart.'

Jader cringed. 'Oh, hell,' he said.

'It turned out that, three or four years earlier, Torquil had been over to stay with some high-society friends of his in Paris,' Ellen carried on tautly. 'While he was there, he met my mother who was dining with an acquaintance of his friends at the same restaurant. He declared she was the most beautiful woman he'd ever seen and that he'd fallen in love at first sight.'

She picked at the loose thread on her jeans. 'Torquil's friends let him ramble on for a while about how he intended to sweep her off her feet and make her marry him, but eventually they explained that she'd been hired for the night. According to Priscilla, her brother was told, with much hilarity, that he didn't need to trouble himself with marriage in order to make the dream girl his; all he required was his credit card.'

'That would do nicely, thank you?' Jader said tersely.

'You got it. While he'd been drooling, Torquil had insisted on having his photograph taken with my mother,' Ellen continued. 'He'd forgotten about it, but one day he came across the packet of Paris snaps and showed them to his sister. Vivienne had used a different working name, but Priscilla recognised her from parents' evenings.

'At first, I was outraged by her claim and furiously denied it,' she said, frowning as she recalled the time which, for years, she had buried deep in her mind. 'I would've denied it with my last breath. I'd always believed my mother had been a showgirl in an exclusive Paris nightclub and I insisted she must've been dining with a man-friend. But when Priscilla stuck to her story and even said she'd get her brother to verify it I started to think.'

A shadow flickered across her face like a cloud. 'I thought of how my mother paid for my private education, of how she'd bought the Kensington apartment where we lived, of her wardrobes of expensive clothes. Granted, she was working at the art gallery—'

'Where she met Conrado when he went in to price a painting,' Jader cut in.

'That's right. Yet Vivienne'd never indicated that she needed to work because she needed the money; it was more a case of her being interested in art and wanting something to do. All things considered, she seemed to be amazingly well off for a showgirl, so—' Ellen paused '—I told her about the photograph and what Priscilla had said.'

His fingers kneaded into her shoulder, as if he was trying to alleviate her pain. 'That must've been difficult.'

'It was. I remember praying I was mistaken and that she'd have some reasonable, respectable explanation which would totally annihilate Priscilla's claim, but Vivienne admitted she'd been a call-girl. She seemed to be relieved I'd found out, because she proceeded to tell me all about it.' Ellen gave a strained smile. 'In gory detail.'

'And how did you feel?' Jader enquired.

'I know it sounds clichéd, but it was as if she'd thrown a hand grenade and blown my life apart. Nothing seemed certain any more. I couldn't trust anyone. My confidence was wrecked. And I hated Vivienne. I was terrified of some past client recognising her and I refused to go out with her and insisted she mustn't ever come to the school again. I also became paranoid about the money she'd spent on me, money which she'd earned in such an awful way. It made me feel dirty.

'But I didn't want my grandparents, or anyone else, to realise something was wrong and start asking questions, so when we were with other people I continued to be amiable.'

'But at home?'

Ellen frowned, remembering. 'For a long time, I would only speak if my mother spoke to me and then I was sullen, but maintaining hatred consumes a lot of energy and gradually I began to act civilly again. Though we never talked about her being a call-girl again. I couldn't bear to talk about it.'

'Were your grandparents never suspicious of her wealth?' Jader asked.

'No. Like me, they believed she was a dancer, though they may have suspected she had some rich man in the background who regularly topped up her finances.'

'They never went over to Paris to see Vivienne in the show?'

Ellen shook her head. 'Although my grandparents were happy to look after me, they had an uneasy relationship with my mother. They didn't approve of her. They felt she'd been a bad influence on my father and they couldn't understand how any mother could abandon her baby.

'When she first went to Paris Vivienne worked as a dancer and she sent photographs. And whenever she visited over the years she would make references to shows and speak of how she'd become a highly paid performer. She even brought pictures which she claimed included her, but one leggy girl in a feathered headdress and shining a glossy smile looks very much like another.'

Jader's brow furrowed. 'Are your grandparents aware of her past now?'

'No, and I shall never tell them,' Ellen vowed. 'They'd be devastated, like Conrado.'

'And like you.'

She gave a grim nod. 'Having to go to school the next day and endure Priscilla's taunts was just about the hardest thing I've ever had to do.'

'You didn't admit she was right?' Jader protested.

'No. I grandly announced that if that was what she wanted to think, so be it. But Priscilla wasn't liked and, after a while, the other girls got fed up with her snide comments and ignored her.'

'But you couldn't ignore the truth about your mother,' he said, and his arm tightened around her. 'Living with it all these years must've been hell.'

'It was,' Ellen replied.

Jader looked at her with concerned brown eyes. 'And it still is?' he enquired.

Her mouth quivered. Tears welled. Her precarious control broke. 'Yes,' she said, and she started to cry.

With her long breath pumping out in harsh sobs, Ellen cried for a long time. She cried for the disgrace, the stress of keeping her mother's sordid secret, for how she—and Conrado—had been made to suffer. She'd believed she had faced up to the demons and put them behind her, but as she wept Ellen recognised that by avoiding any examination of her memory she had denied them. She had told herself she could cope, yet this was the first time she had given any searching thought to the past and the first time she had put her thoughts into words. It had been coping by evasion.

Jader held her close, murmuring words of comfort and rubbing her back. 'My father called you ''poor Ellie'', but it should've been *brave* Ellie,' he said as her gasping sobs began to subside.

Ellen sniffed. 'I'm not brave,' she protested.

'Oh, but you are, *querida*,' he declared, kissing her brow, 'and from now on you will be braver.'

She looked at him. 'I think so,' she agreed, and explained how, for years, she had been blocking out a full acceptance of her mother's history and the impact it had on her. Ellen sniffed again. She felt better. 'Would you mind if I carry on talking?' she asked.

'And continue the therapy? Do.' Lifting a hip, Jader drew a clean white handkerchief from his trouser pocket. 'Here,' he said.

'Thanks.' Ellen blew her nose and wiped her cheeks. 'I must look a mess,' she said.

'You look beautiful, even if your mascara's run and you're a little pink around the nostrils.'

'Flatterer,' she said, and smiled.

'Brazilian,' Jader countered. 'Brazilian men never hide their appreciation of a beautiful woman. Like you, and your mother,' he said, deftly steering her back into talking. 'How did Vivienne become involved in the call-girl racket?' he asked. 'And why?'

'The initial motivation was money,' Ellen replied. 'When my parents married, my father was a chef at a top London hotel, and because he produced some innovative dishes, and was young and good-looking, he was written about in magazines and became a minor celebrity,' she started to explain.

'Vivienne was dancing at this time?' Jader checked.

'Yes, she'd been in the chorus line of a couple of West End musicals and was in a third when they met—though she became pregnant with me a couple of months before they married and gave up work.'

'Was her pregnancy the reason why they married?' he enquired.

Ellen shook her head. 'It brought the date forward, but they were very much in love and had planned to marry anyway. My mother was keen for my father to open his own restaurant,' she went on. 'That was his plan too, though he'd intended to wait a couple of years until he could save more money and was in a better financial position. However, it seems she insisted now was the time and he let himself be talked into it. They found premises which were in a good location, but at a far higher rent than my father had anticipated.' She grimaced. 'Vivienne pushed him to take them and he did.

'Next the restaurant had to be equipped and furnished. According to my grandad, my father had worked out costs and fixed a budget and, at first, he was determined to stick to it, but my mother encouraged him to buy nothing but the best.'

'And he went along with her wishes, because he was so in love with her?' Jader said.

Ellen nodded. 'In order to pay for the expensive kitchen equipment, the silver cutlery, the carpets and fancy curtains, et cetera, he needed to borrow, but he didn't tell her how deeply he had to go into debt.'

'And Vivienne didn't realise?'

'No. Her only thought appears to have been the trendy up-market restaurant which they'd own and the glamour attached to it. The business had been operating for a few months, when my father walked into the road and under a truck. He was twenty-eight. Just two years older than I am now,' Ellen said sadly.

'He was killed because he was worrying about his debts and didn't look where he was going?' Jader enquired.

'My grandparents think so and blame my mother, but it could've been a straightforward accident. Anyway, after his death, all the money he owed came to light. In order to start paying off the debts, the restaurant's fixtures and fittings had to be sold—at a knockdown price,' she said ruefully, 'plus the flat my father had owned, even their car. My mother was stunned. Perhaps it was due to her being in shock after his death, but she decided he'd double-crossed her and let her down.'

'But he went into debt to please her, so you can argue that Vivienne was partly responsible,' he protested.

'True, yet she's always refused to accept it. What made things worse was that some of the money my father had borrowed he'd borrowed from loan sharks. They were nasty characters who sent their heavies round to threaten her. They said she'd get hurt and so would I if she didn't make recompense. My mother was terrified and she blames my dad for that too.'

'She must've found blaming him preferable to blaming herself,' Jader remarked drily.

'Could be,' Ellen agreed. 'She assured the heavies that she'd raise the cash though it'd take her a long time and, after much pleading, they agreed to wait. Not much later, she saw an advertisement for a dancer in Paris which paid well, applied and got the job.'

He frowned. 'Vivienne didn't consider taking you with her to Paris?'

'No. She asked my grandparents if they'd care for me, initially for twelve months, while she made money to help pay off the debts. But she isn't a motherly person and I doubt the prospect of handing me over troubled her too much.' Ellen gave a wry smile. 'She may even have been thankful.

'At the start, the amounts she paid off were small, but within three years the total sum had been cleared—thanks to someone noticing her in the floorshow and talking about her to Madame Lydie.'

'She recruited your mother?' Jader asked.

Ellen nodded. 'Madame ran a call-girl service which provided elegant young women for clients such as ambassadors, business tycoons, Middle Eastern princes.'

'So when Vivienne travelled she was travelling to meet them?'

'Yes. Some of Madame Lydie's clients had weekly standing orders and the girls were flown in on royal flights. As my mother told it to Conrado, during those years she was working in the art trade and selling paintings, but in reality—' Ellen clutched his handkerchief tight in her fist '—she was selling herself.'

'Madame must've danced a jig when she saw Vivienne,' Jader remarked acerbically.

She nodded. 'The special thing about her girls was that they looked exactly the same as the loveliest well-bred young women and fitted perfectly into society. Her first criterion was that they must be beautiful, with a slender figure and fine manners. My mother passed with full marks, but she had to learn how to behave in the grandest of company and was sent to study languages and told to read certain books. The girls were expected to be able to talk knowledgeably and amusingly to their customers, as well as being good in bed.'

'Vivienne wasn't deterred by the sexual side of the transaction?'

'She enjoyed it.'

Jader looked at her with level brown eyes. 'Like you enjoy sex,' he said.

'I enjoy it—with you,' Ellen told him jerkily.

'Not before?' he queried.

'Not as much. Not nearly as much. My previous partners weren't as...sensually aware as you, but, in any case, I felt inhibited and self-conscious and unable to relax.' She frowned. 'I think I was afraid of being thought wanton.'

'You were scared of drawing what you saw as a parallel between you and Vivienne?' Jader demanded. 'Ellen, it's one thing to share passionate love with a man you're attracted to and whom you have chosen, and quite another to engage in sex with a stranger for cash.'

'I know that. Now.'

'You were enchantingly wanton with me,' he said, and his gaze fell to settle on the soft fullness of her lips.

Ellen's heartbeat accelerated. Jader was going to kiss

her and she wanted him to kiss her. But as he began to lean towards her he appeared to undergo a last-minute change of mind and he straightened.

'You said your mother's initial motivation in working as a call-girl was money,' he recalled. 'But after she'd paid off the debts?'

'She did it for personal gain and her own pleasure.'

Jader uttered an oath. 'Pleasure?' he protested.

'Working for Madame Lydie had meant instant elevation into a rich, jet-set world which she found glamorous. Her clients may not have been either young or attractive, but they invariably had status,' Ellen told him, 'and that excited her.'

'If it was such a great life, why on earth did she stop?' he demanded brusquely.

'Partly because she was getting older, partly because she had ample cash in the bank, and partly because an art dealer, who wasn't a client but who knew she worked for Madame Lydie, offered her a job in his London gallery and she was ready to come back. She also felt it was time she settled down with someone.'

'I assume ''settling down'' didn't include having any more children?' Jader enquired.

'Vivienne couldn't have any more. When she was in Paris she'd had a mishandled abortion which had left her unable to conceive.' Ellen gazed down at the handkerchief she held in her hand. 'Which was another reason why I felt it'd be unfair for her to marry Conrado.'

'He didn't realise she couldn't have children?'

'No. From time to time, he'd make some comment about how much he would like to have a second family, but whenever he did she would just smile.'

Jader's jaw tightened. 'So Vivienne deceived him about that, and about her wealth. Conrado was under the impression your father had died just a few years earlier and that he'd left her the apartment and plentiful funds.'

'I realised that,' Ellen said. 'But even if she deceived him she did love him, as much as she was capable of loving any man. You talked of her having a core of sadness, but to me it seemed an empty core. After my father was killed, when Vivienne decided he'd cheated her, she seemed to lose faith in love.'

'She'd been so hurt by him, as she saw it, she resolved never to be hurt by a man again?' he said pensively. 'That could go some way to explaining her acceptance of being a call-girl.'

'You mean she was getting back at men by making them pay for her favours?' Ellen mused. 'Could be.'

'How did Vivienne react to the split with my father?' Jader enquired.

'She was very upset. Before they'd met she'd had a busy social life, though she never talked about her escorts because they didn't appear to interest her that much. But, after Conrado, it was over a year before she went out with anyone again.'

'And she doesn't love her husband?'

'No, though she's fond of him,' Ellen said. 'Bernard knows it and he accepts it.'

'Conrado would never have settled for "fond"; he would've needed Vivienne's complete devotion,' Jader declared, and frowned. 'His silence about her being a call-girl demonstrates how repugnant he found it. Hell, he couldn't even manage to bring himself to tell me.'

'Knowing the woman you love has sold herself for cash isn't an easy thing to reveal,' she said, 'to anyone.'

'Nor is revealing that your mother sold herself,' he said gravely.

'No.' For a moment, Ellen rested her head on his shoulder, then she drew back. 'But what doesn't kill you is said to make you stronger, and I'm still alive. You were going to ring São Paulo,' she said, suddenly remembering. 'Suppose I get you the number and then, as it's gone six, make us a drink to take out onto the terrace? What'll you have—the usual soda?'

'Please.' Jader's mouth curved. 'We're getting to be like an old married couple,' he remarked as she rose to her feet. 'Except that you're a career girl.'

She turned back to him. 'A dedicated one,' she declared.

As he greeted his associate, Ellen took the tray of dirty pots through to the kitchen. She stacked the dishwasher, then made a detour into her bedroom to wash her face. Thank goodness she had not been looking at Jader when he had made his 'married couple' comment, she thought as she flannelled the mascara from her cheeks. It had sliced into her like a knife, and he could have recognised her sudden agitation and perhaps sensed the wild beating of her heart. Yet it had been a casual comment which he had instantly dismissed. Ellen made a face at herself in the mirror. She must dismiss it too.

As she took their drinks outside, Jader completed his call and followed her onto the terrace. Sipping at his soda, he talked about how his sustained absence from the São Paulo office would allow his second-in-command to flex his business muscle, but, inevitably, he eventually returned to their earlier conversation.

'You rebelled against Vivienne's past by becoming a plain Jane,' Jader stated.

Ellen nodded, acknowledging the connection he had made. 'Although it was subconscious, I think that for a long time I had a horror of giving off any kind of sexual signal in case *I* was identified as a tart and so I went out of my way to be dowdy.' She sipped at her wine. 'With hindsight, I suspect I was also getting back at my beautiful mother by being this horrendously unattractive daughter.'

'Ease up,' he protested. 'You weren't that bad.'

'I didn't make your heart go pitty-pat,' Ellen said.

'No, not then, but you were sixteen and still at school, whereas I considered myself to be a sophisticated man about town,' he said drily. 'Yet despite the dental wire and the grungy clothes and the hacked-off hair you were a sweet sixteen.'

Ellen said a rude word.

'I mean it,' Jader insisted, and grinned. 'You possessed the appealing air of a small, cuddly animal struggling to escape from a potato sack.'

She laughed. 'Gee, thanks.'

He took another mouthful of soda. 'How do you feel about Vivienne now?'

'It's complicated,' Ellen said thoughtfully. 'She forfeited the mother and child bond long ago and I'm much closer in that way to my grandma, yet Vivienne *is* my mother.'

'So you love her?'

'Yes, and in an odd way I feel protective of her—though I don't approve of her morals and I resent her abandoning me. Like I told you, I was happy with my grandparents, who are lovely people, but they weren't young and they looked like grandparents. I was always conscious of that and I wanted so much to be a member of a proper family, with a mum and a dad.'

She paused. 'Conrado recognised my need. I'm sure he also recognised that I *had* to alert him to the truth about my mother's past and, no matter how much it hurt him, he was grateful and he left me the shares in acknowledgement.'

'And in thanks for allowing him his second family.'

Reaching out, Jader ran his knuckles softly down her cheek. 'When he spoke about you, Conrado's eyes would grow misty and now I understand why. He knew what you were going through.'

Ellen blinked. Her eyes were misting too. 'I think so,' she said chokily.

'It's not only call-girls who sell themselves for cash,' he said, sitting back. 'Read the international press and you read of women who make a career out of moving from one rich man to the next, who stake out millionaires and go all out to entrap. You could argue that their morals aren't so different to those of a call-girl, or are even worse.'

'I suppose so,' she agreed.

'And, after the uncaring childhood Vivienne seems to have suffered, followed by the untimely death of your father, maybe we shouldn't condemn her too harshly?'

Ellen nodded. After years of trauma, a calmness was seeping into her. A calmness which Jader had made possible.

'Thank you for being so understanding,' she said.

CHAPTER NINE

HER knees lifting and her elbows moving like smooth-oiled pistons, Ellen ran at a steady pace. On the far side of the water, golden rays of early morning sun were gilding the forested mountains. A bird sang somewhere. Dragonflies played darting games of hide-and-seek against a pale blue sky. She breathed in, breathed out. The air was cool and fresh, with a faint fragrance of blossom. Her sense of well-being surged. To be running beside the lagoon, on a tranquil morning and in such a lovely setting, was invigorating.

She glanced at Jader who jogged rhythmically beside her. Clad in a pair of brief black shorts and trainers, he looked virile, athletic and fit.

'How—are—the ribs—and—shoulders?' Ellen panted.

He rolled the shoulder in question, then ran a hand around his golden, hair-sprinkled chest. 'Everything's feeling fine,' he reported, and they smiled at each other.

Ellen maintained her stride. Her wish had finally come true: she and Jader were friends. They talked comfortably and for hours together, enjoyed much shared amusement, managed the mechanics of day-to-day living together with remarkable ease. She wiped away a slick of moisture from her brow. Their relationship would have been one of perfect rapport, if it had not been for the physical aspect—which was non-existent.

Although three weeks ago Jader had been quick to advise her that his injuries did not necessarily mean a total shut-down of their sexual alliance, ever since he had maintained a careful distance. And placed an embargo on any remark which could be construed as even faintly provocative.

Common sense insisted that she should be grateful, because this was, after all, what she had wanted—except that she did not want it now. Ellen accepted that she was operating on instinctive need rather than intellect, but she longed for Jader to touch her, to kiss her, to make love to her—at least once more before she left. Her fingers curled, her nails biting into her palms. She longed for it with a passion. She was becoming *obsessed* by longing.

Initially, she had wondered whether his strapped chest might be troubling him, dissuading him, for, whilst Jader still required her to shave him, help dress him—*touch* him—he never touched *her*. And although his movements had become freer with time he'd made no advances. A couple of days ago she had driven him to the hospital where all bandages had been removed and his bones had been pronounced healed. For forty-eight hours she had been in a froth of expectation—surely now he must act?— but their relationship remained platonic.

Ellen pounded on. What made the situation even more screamingly frustrating was that Jader longed for her as much as she longed for him. She had seen his desire smouldering in the darkness of his eyes when he had not realised she was looking at him. She could hear it in the husky timbre of his voice. She had noticed it in the tensing of his body when she came close. It was glaringly obvious that she continued to drive him crazy, yet his resistance had become implacable.

Why? Ellen's heart went cold. Because Jader was now aware of her mother's history. He might have been sympathetic and understanding when she had told him the unsavoury details—indeed he remained sympathetic and understanding, for they had talked about the matter on several occasions since—yet it had brought about a change in his feelings. Whilst he was willing to be a friend, he preferred to avoid anything deeper. Jader had not outlawed her from his life, like her journalist boyfriend, Ellen thought bleakly, but now he harboured reservations about her.

She frowned out across the sun-glittered water. The ironic thing was that whilst Jader found this a problem she no longer did. Talking through her mother's secret had enabled her to accept it. OK, she would not be using the topic as a conversation opener—or stopper—at parties, Ellen thought drily, but she could face it head-on. The insecurity which she had attempted to mask and deny for so many years had gone.

They ran the distance they had decided upon and, with the sun rising higher in the sky, jogged more casually back to the apartments.

'That made the adrenalin pump,' Jader remarked as they entered the lift. He pressed the button for his floor. 'I've missed being able to exercise.'

'It was good,' Ellen agreed. 'Better than running at home,' she continued as they started to ascend.

She was explaining how her regular circuit was a tour of the back streets around her small Fulham flat, when she suddenly realised she was chattering guilelessly away while Jader was standing in silence, gazing at her. She tensed. The brooding look in his dark eyes made her nerve-rackingly aware of them being together in the confined space—with him handsome, lean and half-naked, and her wearing a cut-away vest and very short shorts. Ellen snatched in a breath. The atmosphere had become so incendiary that if a match was struck it seemed everything might explode.

'You may reckon I'm watchable, but I would be obliged if you'd stop looking at me like that,' she said, annoyed that he should have alerted her to his sex appeal, and irked by their mutual unfulfilled desire.

'Like what?' Jader asked.

'You know.'

'I don't,' he said, picking up her mood and speaking sharply. 'Tell me.'

Ellen wafted a cross hand. 'Oh, forget it.'

'No, I bloody won't,' he said, with some heat, then the anger drained out of him. 'Sorry. I've not been sleeping too well these past few nights,' he told her as the lift came to a halt, 'and I guess I'm a bit tetchy.'

'Ditto,' she said.

They were walking into the apartment, when Jader tilted his head. 'Telephone,' he declared, and strode off to answer it.

Going into her room, Ellen shed her running clothes, pulled on a shower cap and went to shower. So Jader was having broken nights too, she thought wryly a few minutes later as she towelled herself dry. Each night, she tossed and turned for what seemed endless hours, imagining her erstwhile lover lying in his bed on the other side of the hall. She had been tempted to join him, but what would happen then—might his reservations about her crumble or would Jader order her away?

Removing the shower cap, Ellen brushed through her hair. Perhaps tonight she should climb into his bed and find out. If she did not try, she would never know, she reflected—and time was running short for in three days she flew home.

Ellen started to dress. Jader might have his reasons for

keeping his distance, but, as he had once said, she was a fighter, so why didn't she fight back? As he was punishing her, why didn't she punish him? Though if they made love it would be a joyous kind of punishment. Ellen was toying with the idea of embarking on a seduction, when Jader strode at full tilt into the room.

'Two pieces of great news! First, that was a call from an American television producer who runs a motoring programme which is aired throughout the States,' he said delightedly, then abruptly broke off.

His need to share his news had brought him to her door and propelled him inside, but his frown made it clear that he had not expected to find her in a low-cut bra and high-cut briefs. On the point of reaching for her robe, Ellen stopped. Whilst Jader might prefer to erase the memory, he had been her lover and she was damned if she would act the coy maiden at this late stage, she thought defiantly. Besides, if she was unsettling him—serve him right!

'And?' she prompted, standing straight and looking steadily back.

'Er—the programme also goes out on Latin American channels, plus international satellite. Apparently the guy spoke to the factory and they gave him my number,' Jader carried on, gathering speed as his enthusiasm outran his discomposure. 'He's read about the Moreira and he wants to feature one in his next series, under the heading of world-class cars for a world market, and we've arranged that he'll send a crew out to Rio next week.'

Ellen laughed. 'Brilliant!'

'Wait for it. The second piece of news is that when I rang the sales manager to advise him of the shoot he told me that Roscoe Chard had been on the phone to say he'd like to buy *two* convertibles, one for here and one for use in the States.'

She laughed again. 'Good old Mr Wonderful!' she declared, and flung herself at him and hugged him.

'It's amazing how things have begun to snowball,' Jader said, wrapping his arms around her. 'Sales are already up and there've been several hundred enquiries, but international TV exposure could mean the factory going into full production and staying in full production.' He grinned. 'Thanks to you.'

'Thanks to us,' Ellen said, and, reaching up, she kissed him lightly on the lips.

Like her hug, the kiss was spontaneous and friendly, but as she pressed close she felt the heat of his bare chest against her and the rub of his skin. Ellen's pulses juddered. She was also aware of Jader becoming aroused.

'I must shower,' he declared, drawing away and taking a step towards the door.

'I'd make it a cold one,' Ellen said pertly.

Jader scowled. 'I guess,' he muttered, and turned to go again.

'Do you like my new underwear?' She rippled a hand down from her amber silk and lace bra to the matching panties. 'I treated myself yesterday when I went shopping for souvenirs to take home. Do you approve?'

Forced to stop again, he cast her an impatient look. 'Very pretty.'

'No more plain Jane,' Ellen announced.

'I guess not,' Jader mumbled. There was the sound of the front door being opened. 'There's Teresa,' he declared, with transparent relief, and disappeared out into the hall.

After dressing in a maize-yellow T-shirt and shorts, which had been another of her purchases of the previous day, Ellen went through to the kitchen. She greeted Teresa and plugged in the coffee-pot. She always spoke to the woman in Portuguese and now understood most of what she said.

'Sorry they've taken so long, but these are for you,' Teresa said, delving into a carrier bag and handing her the snaps she had taken of them at the Carnival. 'I've already given the *senhor* his set. I take good photographs, yes?' she demanded.

'Very good,' Ellen agreed. 'And thank you.'

In truth, the shots had been over-exposed and were slightly blurred—though she suspected she might well spend much of the rest of her life gazing at them nevertheless.

'And these are of my daughter and her samba school,' Teresa said, taking out several packets.

She proceeded to proudly show Ellen endless snaps and, as she had done before on several mornings, launched into a lament that the school had not won, followed by the stout declaration that it would do so next year. It was only when Jader appeared that Teresa remembered she was there to clean and rushed off to attend to the bedrooms.

'When you spoke to the factory, did you arrange for my signature to be witnessed on the sale form?' Ellen asked as they were eating breakfast. 'Either me going to them or them coming here?'

Jader shook his head. 'I forgot.'

'Again? But I've been asking you to fix it for ages,' she protested. 'I could've signed when you took me around the plant a couple of weeks back, only you said there was no hurry. But now there is.'

'If you keep the shares, they're going to increase in value and could increase substantially,' he said. 'It makes sense to hang on for a while.'

Ellen gave a taut smile. It might make financial sense, but if she retained her shares in the car company she would be retaining an ongoing connection with him. And when she left Brazilian shores she wanted to leave Jader de Sa Moreira behind her and start the process of emotional recovery.

'I need the money from the shares so that I can open my own office,' she declared. 'It's the ideal chance for me to get started.'

'My advice is still to wait,' Jader said tersely.

'I don't want to wait,' Ellen insisted.

He sighed. 'I'll get things organised some time today,' he said, and rose to his feet. 'Time to go to work.'

Every morning, while Teresa cleaned and washed and ironed, they spent a few hours dealing with their respective businesses. Seated at the bureau in the living room, Jader would call his management in São Paulo and at the car plant, and discuss trade, make decisions, sometimes dictate letters to a secretary. Meanwhile, sitting at the kitchen table, Ellen wrote up the notes on Rio which she had made the previous day, added extra observations, drafted articles.

Today, as she leafed through her notepad, Ellen sighed. Her enthusiasm for opening an office had been fake. Maybe she would feel keener once she was back home, but, right now, she did not care. She ran a fingernail along the spiral binding of her pad. Gathering information and taking photographs had lost its appeal too. Over the past three weeks, Jader had gone out of his way to help. He had taken her into the *flavelas*, out to the islands, alerted her to different issues, introduced her to all manner of fascinating people. He had also insisted on buying her several reference books.

Ellen made a face. Ask her a question about Rio and chances were she could answer it, but writing and marketing her articles no longer held much interest.

Picking up a ballpoint pen, Ellen dutifully though halfheartedly transcribed her notes. The work session progressed, but as soon as Teresa left she cleared away her files. They would be having cold roast chicken for lunch and she started assembling a salad to accompany it.

'This afternoon I suggest we go out across the Niterói Bridge,' Jader said, walking into the kitchen.

'Thanks, but I'm up to here——' Ellen raised a hand to her neck '——in reels of film and information about Rio. I can't face any more. I intend to take things easy from now on and I'd like to top up my tan.'

He looked surprised, but he shrugged. 'Which beach would you like to go to?'

'No beach. I'd prefer to sunbathe here,' she told him.

'Here?' Jader protested.

'Out on the terrace on one of the loungers.' Ellen cut tomatoes into quarters. 'If you don't mind?'

'I don't mind,' he declared.

'There's no need to stay with me,' she said. 'If you want to go to the factory, please do.'

Jader shook his head. 'I have some business reading which I need to catch up on.'

After lunch, Ellen changed into her topaz bikini, rubbed in sun oil, and went out onto the terrace. Jader was already installed at the table, in the shade of an umbrella. He wore a short-sleeved shirt and shorts, and was looking through a pile of papers. Walking past him, she spread out her towel on the padded lounger and sat down. For a while, Ellen read a paperback which she had brought, then she reached into her bag.

'Would you do my back?' she asked, holding out a bottle of tanning oil. She smiled. 'Please.'

A line cut between his brows and there was a moment when it seemed as if Jader might refuse, but then he nodded. Rising to his feet, he took the bottle from her, unscrewed the cap and poured a small pool of golden oil into his palm. As Ellen lay down on her stomach, he bent and began to rub the top of her back. She closed her eyes. The slippery sweep of his fingers over her skin was tinglingly erotic.

'Wait,' she said as his hand moved between her shoulderblades, and, lifting herself up and reaching behind, Ellen released her bra top. When she lay down again, the smoothly swelling sides of her breasts were visible.

'You're not making things easy for me,' Jader said curtly.

Abruptly angry, Ellen twisted around and sat up. She had had enough of pretence. She was sick to death of the fiasco.

'I'm supposed to?' she demanded, glaring at him. 'That's rich! And am I also supposed not to notice how—?'

'Are you doing that on purpose?' he rasped.

'Doing what?' Ellen enquired, and lowered her eyes in the direction of his gaze. When she'd sat up so furiously, she had spread a hand to hold her bikini top in place, but one side had drooped, exposing a perfectly round breast topped by a pinkly pouting nipple. 'No, I'm not,' she said, though she made no attempt to cover herself up, 'but there's no need to panic.'

Jader stood upright. 'Panic?' he questioned, frowning down at her.

'I've noticed how you don't like being alone with me in private too much and how you avoid any situation where we might get too close. But if we do, if we should end up in bed together—did somebody's blood run cold?' Ellen flung at him. 'It's not the end of the world, even if you do consider I'm tainted.'

His brow furrowed. 'Tainted?'

'Whilst you've been very supportive about Vivienne, get down to the nitty-gritty and you don't want to be associated with a whore's daughter.'

'Yes, I do,' Jader protested.

'Not on an intimate level. Before ignorance was bliss, but now—' Ellen gave an aimless shrug. As abruptly as it had flared, her anger was spent, replaced by *tristesse*. 'I understand,' she said. 'It's happened before.'

'You mean when you told your boyfriend about Vivienne it…damaged your relationship?' he hazarded.

'It was the kiss of death,' Ellen said, and, bending over, she hooked on her bikini top and fastened it. 'I told him in a weak moment because I felt I needed to confide in someone. We'd been going out together for almost a year and he said he loved me—'

'Did you love him?' Jader interrupted.

'No, though I believed I was moving that way,' Ellen replied. 'Anyhow, I told him thinking he'd lend a kindly ear, only to discover that knowing about my mother's activities fell way out of his comfort zone. He'd been all set to take me to meet his parents and wanted us to become engaged, but the idea of introducing me to Mummy and Daddy was ditched, and as for an engagement—forget it! He never asked me out again and when he was forced to speak to me at work it was clear he considered me to be trash.'

Her backbone straightened. 'I am not trash. Yes, I've inherited my mother's genes and come from the same bloodline, but I am *me*. I do not consider I'm tainted—'

'Neither do I,' Jader said.

'Come on,' Ellen protested. 'For the past three weeks you haven't touched me.'

'For the past three weeks I've been thinking about how

keen you are on your career and warning myself against pushing you into a relationship too soon.'

She cast him a suspicious glance. She refused to be bamboozled. 'Explain,' she demanded.

Drawing round his chair, Jader sat down facing her. 'I was well aware that when we came back from the Carnival ball, before we made love, you had doubts about it,' he said.

'You were?'

He inclined his head. 'I believe it's called received awareness,' he said drily. 'But I ignored your doubts and kissed you and—well, we both know what happened next. And again, when we made love in the car, I didn't give you a choice.'

'I could've refused,' Ellen said.

'But you didn't, because you're just as…sexually wild about me as I am about you. However, you've made it clear how ambitious you are and I respect that because I'm ambitious myself,' Jader carried on. 'You came to Rio because the trip would be useful to your career and—'

'No,' she broke in. 'I came because of you.'

Jader's dark brows lowered. 'Me?'

'Yes. I wanted us to be friends.'

'And we are. But your career matters to you,' he went on, 'so when I realised that you mattered to me things got screwed up.'

Ellen felt a fugitive moment of joy. 'I matter to you?' she asked.

'So damn much! Why do you think I stayed on in Rio after I smashed myself up, rather than going home?' Jader demanded. 'Why do you think I asked you to stay and look after me? Why do you think I pretended to be so helpless when my arm was in the sling?'

'You weren't helpless?' she protested.

'Not that much, but I needed you close to me, even if it was a kind of torture—which is why I haven't gone back to work earlier. I needed to be with you and, heaven knows, I wanted to make love to you. I love you,' Jader said, his eyes so dark with emotion that they were almost black.

Ellen looked at him. Her joy was growing, blossoming, billowing. 'You do?' she said.

'With all my heart, *querida*.'

She placed her hand on his knee. 'I love you too,' she told him.

'Thank goodness,' Jader said hoarsely.

'You didn't guess?' Ellen asked, her eyes dancing.

He grinned. 'I had a strong suspicion—but I don't want to push you into a commitment which you might later regret,' he continued seriously. 'I've been too damned domineering in the past and I'm determined not to dominate again. Which doesn't mean I don't hope that once you've dedicated a couple of years to your career you'll decide you'd rather settle for me. I do.

'That's why I've delayed fixing for you to sell your shares,' he went on. 'OK, I'm being selfish, but if you keep them it means we keep in touch. And I can give you the money to set up an office. I can also come over to England and you can come back here and—' Losing patience with himself, Jader threw up his hands. 'The boot is finally on the other foot,' he said.

She frowned. 'Translation?'

'Women have suggested marriage to me, but this is the first time it's been what I want.'

Her joy wrapped itself around her like a warm, snug cloak. 'Are you proposing?' Ellen enquired.

'I am,' Jader said, and moved to sit on the lounger beside her. 'I'm prepared to wait, for a year or two, but—'

'I'm not prepared to wait,' she told him, 'and, as for my career, I can continue it here.' She grinned. 'Until we have our first baby.'

'So you will marry me?'

Hooking an arm around his neck, Ellen rubbed her lips over the rough texture of his recently shaved cheek. 'Yes, please, *querido*,' she said.

Jader kissed her, long and lovingly and deeply, then he placed his arm around her and drew her upright.

'We may've made love in the car and we could make love on the lounger, but I'd prefer the long, slow comfort of a bed,' he told her.

Ellen smiled into the eyes of the man who was her good friend, her perfect lover and would soon be her beloved husband.

'Whatever you wish,' she said, and together they walked from the terrace.

The world's bestselling romance series.

HARLEQUIN®
Presents

Seduction and Passion Guaranteed!

Introducing Jane Porter's exciting new series

THE *Galván Brides*

**The Galván men: proud Argentine aristocrats...
who've chosen American rebels as their brides!**

IN DANTE'S DEBT
Harlequin Presents #2298

Count Dante Galván was ruthless—and though it broke Daisy's heart she had no alternative but to hand over control of her family's stud farm to him. She was in Dante's debt up to her ears! Daisy knew she was far too ordinary ever to become the count's wife—but could she resist his demands that she repay her dues in his bed?

On sale January 2003

LAZARO'S REVENGE
Harlequin Presents #2304

Lazaro Herrera has vowed revenge on Dante, his half brother, who refuses to acknowledge his existence. When Dante's sister-in-law Zoe arrives in Argentina, it seems the perfect opportunity. But the clash of Zoe's blond and blue-eyed beauty with his own smoldering dark looks creates a sexual force so strong that Lazaro's plan begins to fall apart....

On sale February 2003

**Pick up a Harlequin Presents® novel and you will enter
a world of spine-tingling passion and
provocative, tantalizing romance!**

Available wherever Harlequin books are sold.

HARLEQUIN®
Makes any time special ®

Visit us at www.eHarlequin.com

HPGALVAN

International bestselling author

SANDRA MARTON

invites you to attend the

WEDDING *of the* YEAR

Glitz and glamour prevail in this volume
containing a trio of stories in which
three couples meet at a
high society wedding—and
soon find themselves
walking down the aisle!

Look for it in November 2002.

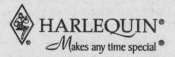

HARLEQUIN®
Makes any time special®

$ Saving Money $
Has Never Been
This Easy!

Just fill out and send in this form from any
October, November and December 2002 books
and we will send you a coupon booklet worth a
total savings of $20.00 off future purchases of
Harlequin and Silhouette books in 2003.

Yes! It's that easy!

I accept your incredible offer!
Please send me a coupon booklet:

_____
Name (PLEASE PRINT)

_____
Address   Apt. #

_____
City   State/Prov.   Zip/Postal Code

In a typical month, how many
Harlequin and Silhouette novels do you read?

❏ **0-2**   ❏ **3+**

097KJKDNC7   097KJKDNDP

Please send this form to:
In the U.S.: Harlequin Books, P.O. Box 9071, Buffalo, NY 14269-9071
In Canada: Harlequin Books, P.O. Box 609, Fort Erie, Ontario L2A 5X3

Allow 4-6 weeks for delivery. Limit one coupon booklet per household. Must be
postmarked no later than January 15, 2003.

HARLEQUIN®
Makes any time special®

Silhouette®
Where love comes alive™

© 2002 Harlequin Enterprises Limited   PHQ402